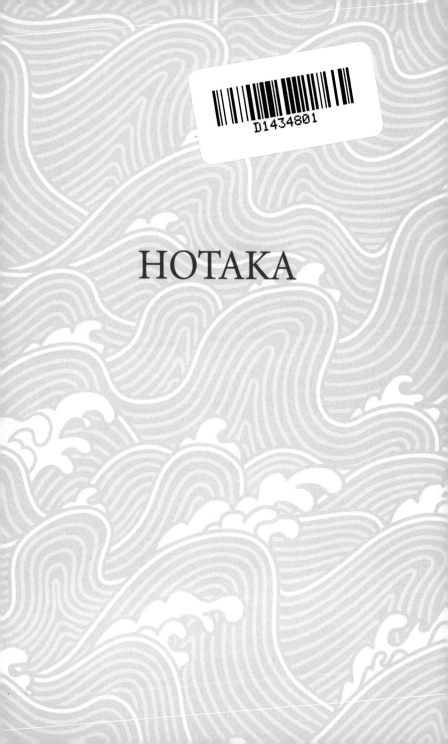

# HOTAKA

**THROUGH MY EYES:
NATURAL DISASTER ZONES**

Hotaka (Japan)

Shaozhen (China)

Lyla (New Zealand)

Angel (Philippines)

**THROUGH MY EYES**

Shahana (Kashmir)

Amina (Somalia)

Naveed (Afghanistan)

Emilio (Mexico)

Malini (Sri Lanka)

Zafir (Syria)

**THROUGH MY EYES** NATURAL DISASTER ZONES

series editor Lyn White

# HOTAKA

## JOHN HEFFERNAN

ALLEN&UNWIN

SYDNEY·MELBOURNE·AUCKLAND·LONDON

First published by Allen & Unwin in 2017

Allen & Unwin
83 Alexander Street
Crows Nest NSW 2065
Australia
Phone: (61 2) 8425 0100
Email: info@allenandunwin.com
Web:   www.allenandunwin.com

A Cataloguing-in-Publication entry is available from the
National Library of Australia
www.trove.nla.gov.au

ISBN 978 1 76011 376 6

Teachers' notes available from www.allenandunwin.com

Excerpt on page 2 is taken from *The Seed of Hope in the Heart: March 2014 – Three years from "3.11"* and is used with kind permission of the author, Teiichi Sato.

Excerpt on page 50 is taken from *Facing the Wave: A Journey in the Wake of the Tsunami*, originally published by Pantheon Books, a division of Random House LLC, New York, 2013. Copyright © 2013 by Gretel Ehrlich. Used with permission. All rights reserved.

Cover and text design by Sandra Nobes
Cover photos: portrait of boy by Shuji Kobayashi/Getty; torī gate by Michael S. Yamashita/Getty; tsunami waves by AFP Photography, LLC/Getty; boat by AAP/ Stephen Morrison © 2017 AAP
Set in 11/15 pt Plantin by Midland Typesetters, Australia
This book was printed in December 2016 by
McPherson's Printing Group, Australia.

10 9 8 7 6 5 4 3 2 1

The paper in this book is FSC® certified.
FSC® promotes environmentally responsible, socially beneficial and economically viable management of the world's forests.

*To the people of the Tōhoku Region*

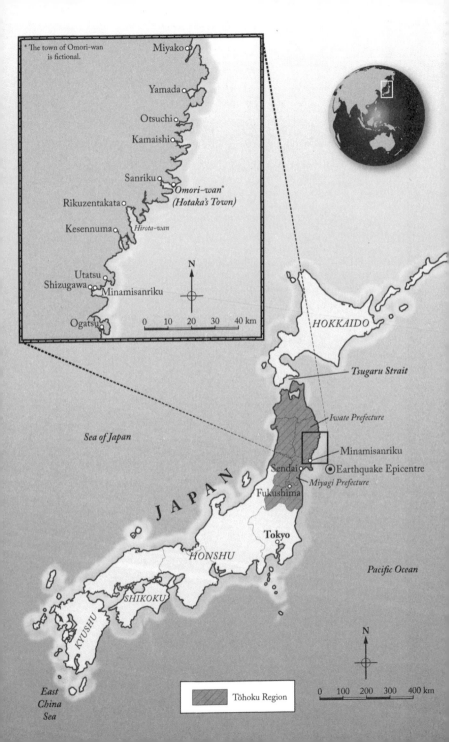

2011

*...the seed of the disaster had been planted and was growing gradually without being detected. Somewhere in the earth, somewhere, the footsteps of an extreme danger were approaching us quietly. Nobody knew that at all. Even experts and researchers of the earthquake did not know. Only the demon of the sea knew it with a creepy smile on its face.*

*The Seed of Hope in the Heart,*
Teiichi Sato, survivor of the 3/11 tsunami
and resident of Rikuzentakata

# One

**'Prepare to die!'**

The young demon-wizard readied himself for combat. His skin flared blood-red and his luminous hair lashed at the air like lightning, as ogres, beasts, ghosts and ghouls hovered menacingly around him. With deadly talons and spiky horns, he kept his foes at bay, waiting for the right moment to attack.

'You don't frighten me!' he snarled. 'I, mighty Oniwaka, will tear you all to shreds and scatter your scraps to the winds. Your end is nigh, cowardly denizens of the deep!'

Oniwaka gave a howl that echoed right through the puppet theatre and set its audience cheering.

'Oniwaka! Oniwaka!' they yelled.

The theatre was packed that afternoon on March 11th for a school matinee, and the air bubbled with excitement as Oniwaka worked himself up for battle. In the front row, Hotaka Yamato was on the edge of his seat. He turned to his best friend, grinning up at him. Takeshi was standing, cheering and shaking his fist at the evil creatures on the screen that made a backdrop to the stage.

Hotaka leapt to his feet as well. 'Destroy them, Oniwaka,' he yelled. 'Destroy the evil ones!'

The bunraku puppet was bigger than most of the young people in the audience, and very lifelike. It even seemed to hear Hotaka, for it leaned over the edge of the stage towards him, shaking a claw-like fist as well and howling the battle cry louder than ever.

The audience loved it. Everyone always loved the shows at the Puppet Palace. They were magical.

The little theatre down by the harbour in the coastal town of Omori-wan was operated by an old couple affectionately known as the Puppet People. Mr and Mrs Suda were famous for their wonderful collection of puppets. He made the faces, bodies, arms and legs, while she sewed the costumes, many of them beautiful pieces of detailed handwork. People came from all over the Tōhoku region to see the Puppet People.

'Prepare to die!' Oniwaka screamed, and leapt at his foes.

Drums rolled, horns blared, cymbals rattled and crashed as the bunraku warrior hurled himself at the screen buzzing with beasts. The battle brought the whole audience to their feet – thumping, stamping, jumping up and down.

Hotaka wanted to leap onto the stage to help the young Oniwaka. If Takeshi had done so he would have followed at once. It was just the sort of thing his best friend would do.

But something else happened instead.

Suddenly everyone stopped – audience, puppets, performers, musicians. They stopped because of a sound that was *felt* more than heard, a sound that moved up through their feet and sent a shudder of dread around the theatre. *Could it be?* For a second everything hung in complete silence. Everyone held their breath, stock still. Listening. Feeling. Waiting.

The answer came in a long, foreboding groan from somewhere deep within the earth. It surged upwards – screeching, grinding, gouging – erupting in a mighty jolt that made the whole theatre lurch like a doll's house kicked by a giant.

'Ji shin, earthquake!' The cry ricocheted through the room as children and adults alike were thrown to the floor.

Everything was shuddering. *Everything* – the chairs, the floor, the ceiling, the curtains, the lights, even the air itself. The walls wobbled and warped. Part of the stage crumpled like cardboard and fell in on itself, bringing down several props. Shelves and cupboards broke off the walls and crashed to the floor. Sections of scaffolding buckled and gave way. One part fell among the musicians, scattering them. Another toppled onto the puppeteers, narrowly missing Mr Suda.

The old man scrambled from the wreckage. 'The doors,' he shouted to his assistants. 'Open them at once, in case they jam, and get everyone outside as quickly as possible.'

The exit that followed could have been an uncontrolled rush if panic had taken hold, with over a hundred people crammed into such a tight space, many of them young. There was still screaming and crying among the youngest, especially when the tremors grew most violent. But the children were well rehearsed in earthquake routine and paid strict attention to their teachers, exiting quickly and in as orderly a fashion as possible.

The earthquake continued right through the evacuation, making the climb up the steep, wobbling stairs out of the theatre extremely difficult. The shaking and juddering went on for over three minutes, far longer than most quakes, only easing in the final stage of the evacuation.

Hotaka and Takeshi were among the last students to leave. At the top of the stairs Hotaka called to Mr and Mrs Suda.

'Thanks for the show,' he shouted. 'I only wish we'd got to see Oniwaka smash those bad dudes.'

'Don't worry,' the old man replied. 'When we've cleaned up the mess we'll have you all back for a replay. Now hurry on!'

# Two

'**Quickly, boys.**'

'Sorry, Abe-sensei,' Hotaka called as he and Takeshi ran to catch the others. 'But the Puppet Man said we could see the rest of the show next week maybe.'

'Can't wait!' Takeshi shouted, punching the air. 'Go, Oniwaka!'

'Yes, of course,' the young sensei, teacher, replied. 'But right now we have to keep moving.'

Miss Abe was Hotaka's favourite teacher, young and happy. She wasn't so happy now, though, he could see, with her brow creased and her eyes darting about for the best way to lead everyone to safety.

'We need to get out of this lane. Tiles could easily fall from the roofs.'

Eight teachers were shepherding the children down the narrow alley from the puppet theatre to a wider street. The main force of the earthquake had eased, but there were still tremors and aftershocks. Electricity poles wobbled and swayed, wires bounced up and down. The lane was badly buckled and crisscrossed with cracks.

There were about a hundred students, walking in pairs, kept to the middle of the lane by the teachers. The buildings in this old part of town were decayed and crumbling. A severe jolt sent a shower of roof tiles raining down. They clattered harmlessly on the pavement but made the smaller children scream.

'Keep together,' one of the teachers cried. 'Keep moving.'

They eventually reached the wider street. Here the traffic was much busier than usual. Some vehicles were heading towards the main road that skirted the harbour, only a block to the east. But most were driving west, into the main part of Omori-wan. The school was that way, about a kilometre past the town centre.

The teachers halted the students at the intersection. Normally they would simply head back to the school, but a few were against this, Miss Abe the main one.

The situation wasn't normal, she insisted; there could easily be a tsunami after such a powerful earthquake and they should get to higher ground immediately. Monk Head Hill was close – down the end of street to the harbour and left. If they walked quickly they could be on safe ground in ten minutes, whereas it would take half an hour to get through town to the school. A tsunami could easily hit in that time.

The older teachers dismissed this. 'There was that strong quake only the other day,' one of them said. 'But no tsunami to speak of. Sirens blared and people were told to prepare for the worst, but nothing happened.'

'But this earthquake was stronger than anything we've ever had,' Miss Abe said. 'And far longer. And it's still not even finished. Surely it's better to be safe than sorry. If there's a big wave, we don't want to be caught in one of the lowest parts of Omori-wan when it hits.'

The older teachers continued arguing. 'It's such a long way around by the hill,' someone said. 'We won't be back at school for ages.' But although they were senior to her, Miss Abe refused to back down, insisting the danger was real.

'I hope I'm wrong,' she said. 'I hope it will be a waste of time going to Monk Head Hill. But I honestly believe the risk is very real. I'm begging you to do this. Please. For the children's sake, please!'

Hotaka saw the anguish on his teacher's face. The other teachers must also have seen it, for they were eventually won over.

'Very well,' they muttered reluctantly. 'Lead on, then.'

Miss Abe gave a sigh of relief and set off at once.

The harbour road was full of cars, trucks, buses and bikes heading north and south, towards the hills that flanked Omori-wan at either end. It looked as though it would be impossible to stop the traffic so that the students might cross to the harbour side of the road, away from the unstable buildings. But Miss Abe stepped boldly onto the road, waving her arms and shouting. Vehicles screeched to a halt in both directions and the teachers quickly directed the students across the road. Once on the other side, Miss Abe gathered them together.

'Listen carefully,' she shouted. 'Especially you little ones. We must get to higher ground without delay.'

The earth rumbled as if warning anyone who might not be listening. Miss Abe pointed to the hill behind her – the one people called Monk Head Hill because much of it was smooth rock, like a monk's bald head. 'Once we're up there we'll be safe. But we must not waste time.'

She turned to the senior students. 'Sixth-graders, I want you to take two little ones each by the hand and lead them up the hill. Follow Kenzo-san. Don't run, but walk as quickly as you can without exhausting anyone. Takeshi, you start – take Rin and little Kumiko. You're next, Yumi, with Ichiro and Riki. Hotaka, you take Yori and Katsu.'

Hotaka headed off with his pair of first-graders, holding their hands tight. For them it was still a kind of adventure, but he knew exactly how serious this was. His grandfather had left him in no doubt about that.

'Always run for the hills after an earthquake,' the old man had told him on many occasions. 'Don't delay. Don't wait around. Get out of the harbour and the lowlands as quickly as you can. A tsunami can travel faster than a bullet train. And don't go back because you've forgotten something. Those who go back never return.'

At that very moment a tsunami warning blared out from loudspeakers at the community centre, while bells rang and sirens sounded in other part of the town. Despite this, some people were actually walking *down* the hill to the harbour, groups of them, to sight-see.

Miss Abe called out to them. 'Be careful. A tsunami is coming.' But they only smiled and continued on their way.

Miss Abe kept the students moving, and they soon reached a point on the hill that the teachers agreed would be above any tsunami. But then other concerns arose. The spot was exposed, an icy end-of-winter breeze hitting it with sleet and even snow. The children were feeling the cold, many of the youngest starting to cry. Two asthmatics were struggling to breathe. Shelter was needed as soon as possible. But where? The teachers were not from this part of Omori-wan, and had no idea where there might be any reasonable shelter for more than a hundred children. The situation was serious.

Hotaka put up his hand. His home was on a road that speared off near the top of the hill and went out to the northern headland of Omori Bay, so he knew this area well. He walked or rode down Monk Head Hill every school morning, and back in the afternoon.

'There's a big family restaurant, Abe-sensei.' He pointed further up the hill. 'It's always open, and there'll be plenty of room.'

'Good work, Hotaka,' the young teacher said. 'Lead the way.'

'I will, if you wish, Abe-sensei. But I have a better idea, if you will allow me to suggest it.'

'Of course, Hotaka.'

'The restaurant is very close, just over the crest; you can't miss it.' Hotaka turned and pointed in the opposite direction, towards the northern headland. 'I can cut across the hill from here and get to my home in about the same time. My mother will be there. She has a car and I know she'll come and help in any way she can. I know she will.'

Miss Abe thought for moment. The condition of the asthmatic children was worsening. Having a car could be invaluable if they needed to be hospitalised. 'Okay, Hotaka. You do that, please.'

'And I'll go with him, Abe-sensei,' Takeshi shouted.

The teacher shrugged. 'Very well then; I suppose two is safer than one. Off you go.'

The boys bowed to their teacher and set off. They walked quickly, in silence. When they were about halfway across the side of Monk Head Hill, Takeshi stopped and peered towards the bay.

'What's happening?' he cried, pointing.

It looked as though the bay was emptying itself, like a huge bathtub, its water draining away. The little river that fed into it was almost dry and the sea bed was visible for about fifty metres from the shore. Several boats were already stranded, while others were being dragged away. Further out in the bay, towards the headlands, some of the big fishing craft were heading to sea. Hotaka peered hard through the sleet, and was pretty sure he saw his Uncle Yori's blue and white trawler leading the fleet.

'Where's the water going?' Takeshi yelled.

'Out to sea,' Hotaka replied. 'Grandpa says it's what happens just before a tsunami hits. The ocean is sucking the bay into its belly. Soon it will spew the lot back at us, and—'

'Ayeee!' Takeshi yelled. 'It's happening now. Look!'

Out in the ocean beyond the headlands, what looked like a thick white line was coming closer. Rapidly closer. Beneath it was something big – no, huge! – and grey.

And then it was there – terrifyingly there.

Hotaka threw his hand to his mouth. 'Nante kotta!' he shrieked. 'What the hell!'

# Three

**A massive wall of water** burst through the headlands and surged across the bay. The wave moved so quickly that Hotaka only just managed to glimpse his uncle's blue and white trawler slide over the top. He heaved a sigh of relief, but then gasped as the stragglers in the fleet were picked up like toys, tossed backwards and swallowed.

Barely half a minute later the wave roared over the breakwater that reached a little way out into the bay, powering on as though it didn't even exist. It hit the marina and grabbed everything in its path – nets, buoys, traps, pots, boats, fuel tanks, gas bottles, machinery, the wharves, the sheds, the *people*. There were no exceptions; the wave took everything and hurled it all at the town.

Hotaka and Takeshi howled in horror. This was a monster like nothing they'd ever seen on TV or in films, or even dreamt of, an unstoppable harvester of death and destruction. It raged on, smashing through the marina wall. People were scrambling from the gridlocked vehicles lined up along the road skirting the harbour, but they didn't have a chance. They were devoured.

Beautiful old buildings along the foreshore were ripped from their foundations and smashed to bits. Quaint houses and rows of shops were flung together in an enormous churning mess that surged on – a giant beast of chaos with an insatiable appetite, feeding as it flowed, gorging itself, grinding, crunching, obliterating all in its path.

The water surged into town, a thickening swill of death, blackened with oil and grime and the grey-green churning of the harbour floor. Voices rose from this roiling spew, cries and shouts and howls for help – victims writhing within the beast itself.

'Nigete, run!'

'Tasukete, help me!'

From where they stood Hotaka and Takeshi could look right across Omori-wan to the hills that rose in the west. But the sleet and snow had become so heavy that they could barely see the town centre, let alone their school. What they saw, though, was more than enough. The wave had reached the centre, its black tentacles slithering through streets, lanes and alleys in search of victims. The surge had slowed, but was still far too fast for anyone on foot.

The boys gaped at the scene of horror spreading around them like some visible disease. 'People are dying!' Takeshi shouted, pointing at the town. 'Dying!' There was anger and outrage in his voice. 'We have to do something!'

'But we told Abe-sensei we'd get help for her.'

14

'What are you talking about? They're safe on the hill. It's down there that people are dying. They're the ones who need help.'

'I know, but what can we do?'

'There must be—' Takeshi choked on his words, his eyes darting about. 'Yes. Over there,' he yelled, pointing down to where the old people's home had stood only minutes earlier.

Most of the building and its occupants had been washed away in the tsunami's initial surge. A piece of decking was still standing, though, buckled and partly submerged. Five people clutched the railing at one end, hanging on for dear life.

'Come on,' Takeshi yelled, and raced down the hill, Hotaka close behind.

When they reached the place, the situation looked dire. The decking creaked and groaned, buffeted by swirling water, in danger of breaking away at any moment. Rescuing these people would be difficult. It was about twenty metres out to the decking; younger, fitter people could swim across, but these were old and infirm. They'd have to be helped. But how?

Among some debris, Hotaka found a length of thick rope, more than enough to bridge the gap. As he untangled it Takeshi secured one end to the stump of a sturdy bush.

'That should hold,' he told Hotaka, tying the other end of the rope around his waist. 'We have to move quickly. If the water rises much more it could sweep away the decking.'

Takeshi was a strong swimmer, and soon reached the decking. He climbed up and bound the rope to the railing, tugging it tight. Then he took the arm of an elderly woman and yelled to Hotaka as he led her towards the edge of the decking.

'I'm bringing her over. Meet me halfway.'

Even though Hotaka knew the water would be perishingly cold, it still took his breath away. The current was stronger than he expected, too, almost pulling his feet from under him. He met Takeshi and took charge of the old woman. She shook with cold and wailed like a frightened child, but Hotaka slowly edged her to shore as Takeshi went back for the next person.

The process was slow and difficult, made even more so by the old people, frail and frightened as they were. One of the men lost his grip as he entered the water; it took all of Takeshi's strength to haul him back to the rope. Then the second-last person, a woman, lunged at Hotaka and clung so tightly around his neck that she dragged him under for a while. He was so exhausted after getting her to shore that he had to rest to catch his breath.

When he turned and started dragging himself out again he saw that Takeshi was in trouble. The last person, a big man, was struggling frantically and had to be hauled every inch of the way.

'I can't swim!' he kept yelling.

As they drew closer Hotaka could see the exhaustion on Takeshi's face. His friend was begging the man to relax, but it made no difference. Hotaka lunged forward, grabbing the old fellow away from Takeshi and was immediately pulled under by the man. He dragged himself by the rope, much of the time submerged, certain he would drown. But just when he thought his lungs would burst, his face broke the surface and he crawled to safe ground, hauling the man with him. Hotaka lay spluttering for a while, then rolled onto his back and stared up at the sky, thankful to be alive.

'We did it!' he shouted, half-gasping, half-laughing. 'We did it, Takeshi.'

There was no reply.

Hotaka sat up and stared around. 'Takeshi?'

His friend was nowhere to be seen.

Hotaka leapt to his feet and screamed, 'Takeshi!'

There was no Takeshi, no sign of him. Just the length of thick rope swaying in the water – the silent unrevealing water.

'Takeshi!' Hotaka dived in and thrashed his way out to the decking, scrambling up onto it. 'Takeshi!'

He scanned the swirling mess, frantically searching. Everywhere. Anywhere. Nowhere. Nothing recognisable. Everything a possibility, but that was all. A voice calling. A hand waving. A head bobbing. Real or imagined? Out there or in his mind? Or both? Nothing was real, everything was a living nightmare.

'Takeshi!'

Hotaka glanced towards the old people. They hadn't moved, all staring at him as if waiting for instructions. Were they stupid? Why weren't they heading up the hill? Another wave could easily come.

'What's the matter?' he shouted. 'Move!' He strode to the edge of the platform. It groaned and tilted more. 'Nigete, get away!'

All moved except the big man who'd been saved last. He didn't budge.

'What's wrong? Are you deaf?' Hotaka screamed. 'Nigete!' The man still didn't move. 'You've got your life. What else do you want? Get out of here!'

But the man began shaking his head, at which a kind of madness gripped Hotaka. He screeched, shook his fists and stamped his feet, so infuriated that he didn't hear the metallic scream. He saw the horror on the big man's face, and felt the lurch beneath his feet.

He was still screaming as the whole deck lifted up and tossed him backwards into the water, then flipped over and slammed down on top of him.

# Four

**Hotaka groaned and rolled over,** wondering where he was but too exhausted to investigate. At least he was alive, he decided; the aches and pains told him that. The light did, too, as little as there was. Life and light went together, didn't they?

But what was that sound?

He had no idea where it was coming from. It could've been in his head for all he knew. That would explain why he couldn't shut it out; it was already *inside* him. Nor could he say *what* it was exactly – a jumble of sounds, nothing definable. Noise.

All he could say for certain was that he hated it. It made his skin creep. Not because it was loud; it was the opposite, in fact. Muffled, as if hidden. Hiding. Like a demon waiting to pounce

And what of the light? It was only a sliver, but it was shining into his eyes. They were already sore, and the light made them sting even more.

So he closed them.

He shouldn't have.

The moment his lids shut, the strange sound exploded. It instantly filled his head – huge and blaring – a freight train in his brain. Screeching, roaring, grinding, shouting, shrieking, squealing, crunching, snarling, crying, yelling, thumping, gnarling, groaning.

He tried to open his eyes, but they were locked shut, imprisoning him in a suffocating blackness that flickered and flared with nightmares. Visions came thick and fast, crowding each other out, spiders scrambling through his mind.

Something grabbed him. A beast? The demon? Whatever it was, it held him down. He struggled, striking out, but the grip tightened.

'Get away,' he yelled.

'Hotaka!'

Tentacles folded around him. Tight. Tighter.

'Leave me alone!'

'It's okay.'

Too tight!

'It's me. You're safe. Safe.'

The voice. He could only just hear it through the noise, but he knew it. The scent, too. And the tentacles were arms, folding around him. He stopped struggling and slowly opened his eyes.

'Okāsan?' He peered up at the face close to his.

'Of course,' his mother whispered. 'Who did you think it was?'

She hugged him so tight that it hurt, her face wet with tears, her body racked by sobs. Eventually she pulled back, holding him at arm's length, smiling and weeping at the same time. A thin shaft of light fell across her face, allowing Hotaka to see the strain and pain etched upon it.

'My beautiful son. You're back with me at last.'

*Back?* Where had he been?

Hotaka was completely confused. He'd just been drowning in a sea of nightmares. Now he was with his mother, aching all over. He gazed about his dim surroundings, gradually realising that the sliver of light was daylight, coming through a slit in some curtains. His bedroom curtains. He looked down at himself; he was in his pyjamas. His bed. Yes, his room. What did it all mean?

That sound in his head was sneaking back, enough to make him shake a little.

His mother noticed. 'You're safe, Hotaka,' she assured him. 'Relax.'

*Relax?* What was she talking about? Impossible.

'There's so much in my head,' he whimpered. 'Bad things, stuff I can't bear thinking about. It's all I can do not to see them, or hear them. They keep creeping up on me. So real and yet too awful to be real.' He grabbed his mother's arm. 'Tell me none of it is real. Say it's all a nightmare. Please!'

His mother reached out and gently stroked his face. 'It's a nightmare, all right. But it is real, I'm sorry to say – a real nightmare that isn't over yet, that will be with us for a long time, I fear.'

She shifted a little so that the light from his window spilled onto a pillow and blanket beside his futon.

'Did you sleep here last night?'

'I had to watch over you. You were in terrible shape, even running a fever. You were shouting, screaming, in and out of consciousness.'

'What do you mean? What happened to me?'

His mother stared incredulously at him. 'Do you remember *anything* about yesterday?'

He shrugged. 'Like I said, my head is full of stuff. Nothing is clear. *Nothing.* It's like static, interference that won't let me think straight.'

'Well, let me tell you this, then. You *almost died* yesterday.'

'*What?*'

'I'd searched everywhere for you, ever since mid-afternoon. I was never going to give up, but as the night wore on I began to prepare for the worst. You weren't found until almost midnight. You were face-down in the mud, barely breathing, hypothermic. The medico said it was a miracle you were alive!'

'Where was I?'

'Down near the harbour.'

Hotaka was having trouble hearing his mother. Sirens sounded, and his whole room seemed to rumble and shake as he tried to piece things together. 'Abe-sensei told us to go home. She took the others.'

'The others? What others? Where did she take them?'

'Up the hill. To safety.' Hotaka stopped, pressing his hands against his head, the pressure becoming too much. 'And then she told us to go home. Just the two of us.'

'Who were you with, Hotaka?'

His mother pressed closer, but it was almost impossible to hear her for the noises in his head.

'*Hotaka.*' Her face was right in front of his. 'Who was with you? Takeshi?'

As soon as his mother said the name, someone screamed it as well. Hotaka heard the scream, and knew it was his own. At the same time, his mother's face was replaced by Takeshi's, blue with cold – only a flash, and then his mother's was there again.

'Was Takeshi with you when the tsunami hit?'

*Tsunami!* The word howled at him.

'Don't know,' Hotaka yelled, struggling with the noise that was everywhere now. 'I think so, yes. But then he wasn't with me.'

'Did he go home?'

'Home?'

'Hotaka! Where did Takeshi go?'

Hotaka struggled to reply, unable to reach the dark place where the answer hid. He stared at his mother, trembling. He could see Takeshi behind her, ghost-like, thrashing about in the swirling thing.

'Don't know!' Hotaka gasped, and collapsed onto his futon, exhausted. 'Don't know.'

'Oh, my boy,' his mother replied, gently stroking his forehead. 'You've been through jigoku.'

She was right, Hotaka thought as her soft fingers lulled him back to sleep. He did feel as if he'd been through some kind of hell. Whether he'd come out the other side, though, he couldn't tell.

# Five

**When Hotaka woke mid-morning,** the vision of Takeshi being swallowed by the tsunami was still in his head. It couldn't be true, he told himself. Takeshi was tough and strong, a fighter. The wave couldn't have taken his life. He was indestructible.

In physical feats there was almost nothing Takeshi couldn't do. He was a standout in several martial arts – judo and karate, but especially kendo. He'd only taken up kendo a year ago and was already beating older guys with his swordsmanship. He was a hit king in baseball, and on the soccer field there wasn't a striker like him. Hotaka was a wing on the same team, and knew that if he could get the ball to Takeshi his friend was bound to score.

Takeshi was such a fighter, too, never giving up. Hotaka recalled the time their team was down two-nil. Takeshi rallied the players at half-time. 'Never say die,' he shouted. They ended up winning. *Never say die!* Takeshi wouldn't have let the wave beat him.

And then there was his diving. He was fearless. He could

actually dive off Eagle Cliff. *Dive!* A thirty-metre sheer drop into the ocean. The best Hotaka could do was jump, and only then from a ledge about halfway down, never from the very top. Takeshi dived without a thought, spearing into the sea like an owashi, a great eagle. That's why he couldn't be gone. He would *never* have let the ocean take him.

'He's still alive,' Hotaka muttered, leaping up and grabbing some clothes. 'And I'll prove it.' He dressed and pulled on his runners. 'I will!'

He scrawled a quick note to his mother – telling her not to worry, explaining that there was something he *had* to do – and climbed out the window.

Hotaka normally loved his walk through the little forest at the back of his house, a winding track beneath a magical canopy of trees. And stepping from the forest onto the side of Monk Head Hill was pure delight, giving a full view of Omori-wan. The town was said to be the prettiest in all of Tōhoku, with its happy mix of quaint and colour-ful buildings along the harbourfront. The scene always made Hotaka smile.

There was no magic this time, though. A grey, drizzly sky cast gloom over everything. There were tremors, too, chilling reminders of what lurked below. But the worst bit of all was what greeted Hotaka when he emerged from the trees. He gasped. He actually cried out, a shriek of pain as if he'd been physically wounded.

There was no Omori-wan.

An army of giants had ravaged the town, kicked and trampled and smashed it to pieces. Small bits were left – pockets to the north and south – but they were few and far between. Hotaka struggled to pick out any landmarks, anything to convince him that this was Omori-wan. Nature had destroyed his town, leaving a scene of utter devastation.

He wandered across the side of Monk Head Hill in a daze, slowly descending, unable to take in the horror that spread before him, yet unable to look away. He was so absorbed by it all that he tripped over something, almost falling. When he glanced back, what he saw made him break into a cold sweat. A stumpy bush. A length of rope trailing away down the hill. Hotaka threw his hand to his mouth and sank to his knees.

Suddenly it was all there. Yesterday. He and Takeshi and the old people. All as clear as could be, and all in complete silence. Nothing to distract, mute images flashing before him, laying out the harsh reality in undeniable, inescapable detail.

Hotaka watched, spellbound, every scene burning into his being. And yet the very last vision of all – the one of Takeshi being sucked down into the abyss – made him leap up and shake his head.

'No! You're wrong. That's not what happened.'

He shouted at himself, at his own mind, for it was doing this. The last time he saw Takeshi, his friend was still afloat. His head was above the water and he was holding the rope. Exhausted, yes. Struggling, yes. But he was there, alive and fighting. At no point did Hotaka actually see Takeshi sucked under. His mind was playing tricks on him.

'You're making it up,' he yelled. 'It didn't happen like that. Takeshi was washed away, that's all. It doesn't mean he's dead.' Hotaka kicked at the bush. 'He's out there,' he yelled, pointing towards the ruins of Omori-wan. 'And I'll find him. I will.'

He strode off, knowing exactly what to do. He'd go to Takeshi's house, if it was still there. It was on the southern side of Omori-wan, and quite a walk. But it made sense to start there and move on if need be. For all he knew he'd find Takeshi with his mother and father. They'd be miserable, like everyone, and Takeshi would be sore and bruised. But he'd be okay. He would! And as bad as things were, they'd laugh. He and his best friend would make each other laugh. That's what they always did.

There were times, Hotaka remembered, when his friend made him laugh until he cried. Takeshi had a neighbour he called Mr Grumpy, who hated children and scowled all the time. The man was probably like that because of the tricks Takeshi played on him. Mr Grumpy was totally bald, and whenever Takeshi got a chance he would open fire on that shiny dome with his pea-shooter. Poor Mr G was sure Takeshi was his attacker, but could never catch him.

Hotaka smiled to himself as he marched down the hill, full of determination. But the closer he drew to town, the worse he felt. By the time he'd reached the harbour his heart had sunk completely.

The beautiful old wharves, once the pride of Omori-wan, were gone, planks and pylons heaped up against the harbourfront, everything smashed and broken. The cobblestone road that ran the length of the old town had been ripped up and washed away. There was mud everywhere, mud mixed with seaweed, wharf decking, pylons, lobster pots, buoys, cars, bikes, trucks, and…and no doubt people. Hotaka shuddered. A large trawler lay on its side, a car crushed beneath it. An even bigger trawler sat perched on top of a three-storey building, one of the very few that hadn't been swept away.

Heavy machinery crunched and growled along the harbourfront – bulldozers and graders, backhoes and excavators, cranes and tractors. Their fumes filled the air, their noise relentless. Hotaka picked his way along the front, dodging machinery, searching for an opening to take him across town. It wasn't easy, for there were no longer streets or roads as such. The old part of Omori-wan had been famous for its narrow alleys, lanes and tree-lined streets, but they were all gone, torn up and buried beneath rubble and debris. Graders and bulldozers were creating new routes, carving them from the chaos.

He eventually found an opening and turned into it. The path was wide enough for traffic in both directions, but there weren't many vehicles, mainly trucks carting rubbish. There were quite a few people, however, some rummaging through the debris. Some had actually found their homes, though how they could possibly recognise anything was beyond Hotaka. He began to have doubts about finding Takeshi's place if that part of town was as badly destroyed as this, but he kept going.

What a scene of suffering and misery, Hotaka thought as he walked, accompanied by a chorus of weeping and moaning. On one corner an old lady addressed a small crowd. Many of them were as old as she was, and they looked frightened and confused. Hotaka had seen the woman before, wandering the streets of Omori-wan. Some said she was a Kitsune, a Fox Woman. Others called her Shaman Lady. Whatever the case, she was supposed to have special powers. Perhaps this was true, for her audience hung on her every word.

'The god Kashima must be angry,' she shouted. 'He has let Namazu whip up the waves of death that have washed our world away.' Some in the crowd nodded earnestly, others wept and wailed. Hotaka shook his head and kept moving.

People wandered aimlessly – lost, dazed, devastated. A woman sat hugging her baby, holding up a photograph: 'Has anyone seen my husband Ichiro?' A man knelt before a pile of debris that must have been his home, head in hands. A staircase rose out of rubble, leading nowhere. A door frame opened onto open air. A cat meowed somewhere. A woman stumbled by with crazed eyes, clutching a doll to her chest. An old man passed. 'Sixty feet,' he shouted like a town crier. 'That's how high the wave was!' He laughed uncontrollably, as if it was all a huge joke. 'Sixty feet!'

Closer to where Takeshi lived, damage from the tsunami was not as bad. There was still a great deal of rubble and debris, and houses had been washed away, but not as many as nearer the harbour. Hotaka was even able to find Takeshi's street; its sign had been bent to the ground by the wave. And to Hotaka's relief, his friend's house was still standing. It had been submerged – the water mark above window height showed that. But it was still standing. Hotaka couldn't help smiling; at least there was hope.

It didn't look as though anyone was there, but he knocked nonetheless, then peered through one of the broken windows and called out. There was no reply. He waited, wondering if there was some way he could leave a note.

'They'd be at the morgue,' someone called from the other side of the street.

Hotaka turned to see Mr Grumpy. 'Where did you say?'

'The morgue, where the bodies are.' Mr Grumpy crossed the street, picking up a shoe that lay in the gutter. 'Well, it's really the gym near the school, but it's been turned into a morgue. Somewhere big enough to lay out all the bodies so people can identify them. They'd be looking for their boy.' He peered at Hotaka. 'You're his friend, aren't you?'

'Takeshi?' Hotaka shouted. 'What makes you say they'd be looking for him there?'

'Well, he didn't come home yesterday, did he? And he wasn't there this morning. Just his parents, and they were crying.' Mr Grumpy almost tossed the shoe onto a nearby pile of rubble, but then thought better of it. 'He'd be gone,' he said, staring down at the shoe, a tremble in his voice.

'You don't know that,' Hotaka snapped. 'He could be lost, he could be hurt. He–he could be *anything*.'

'Okay.' Mr Grumpy backed away, glancing warily at Hotaka. 'I suppose he could. But—'

'Don't say it,' Hotaka yelled, turning his back and rushing away. 'You're wrong!'

# Six

Hotaka hurried off, Mr Grumpy calling after him. He broke into a run, desperate to escape the destruction and the suffocating sadness, but especially the looming realisation that Mr Grumpy was probably right. And then those noises were building in his head again, the visions too, and he knew he couldn't cope if they grew much worse. He ran blindly, bumped into someone and almost fell, but stumbled on, heading west towards the higher part of town.

When he eventually stopped, he was above where the tsunami had reached. Panting to catch his breath, he realised he was next to the town's main Buddhist temple and Shinto shrine. The torī, the huge gate into the sacred area, towered over him. His gaze fell upon the kanetsukidō, the bell house, its four wooden pillars reaching up to a pitched roof. Inside hung the bonsho, a bronze bell about a metre and a half in height. Covered in decorations and inscriptions, the ancient bell gave Hotaka a strange sense of calm and security. He'd heard it said that the Buddha is within the bonsho.

The temple precinct was crowded. People were seeking shelter and comfort there, food and clothes were being distributed, and endless services were being conducted for the dead. Mourners filed by, placing photographs beneath urns of ashes, lighting incense, intoning prayers. Several monks were busy writing ihai, wooden memorial tablets for the dead.

Abbot Etsudo was there, Hotaka noticed. The man was impossible to miss; tall and imposing, he stood out from the crowd in many ways. He was the jūshoku, head of the temple, renowned for his infectious chuckle and big loud voice, although now he was quiet and subdued as he moved around comforting people. Hotaka had met the abbot once or twice with his grandfather, and liked him. He was known as the Jolly Monk because he was happy and tried to make others happy and see goodness in life. How he expected to do that today, though, Hotaka couldn't imagine.

The abbot suddenly looked up and saw Hotaka. He waved and came over.

'Hotaka, isn't it? Fujimoto-san's grandson.' He smiled warmly.

'That's correct, Jūshoku-san. Konnichiwa.' Hotaka bowed.

'How are you, my boy?'

Hotaka shrugged. What could he say?

'I'm sorry, that's a silly question. How would anyone be today? We are all of us lost. Every single one of us. Quite apart from the enormous pain and grief many are suffering, the tsunami has swept away all our bearings, all our anchors, and left us adrift.' The abbot shook his head sadly. 'Tell me, how's that grandfather of yours? Okay, I hope.'

'I'm happy to say that Jīchan is up in the hills staying with his friend Mr Rho for a few days. So he'd be fine. But I'm sure he'll also be really worried and upset and wishing he could be here.'

'Yes, of course. I can't think of anyone who does more to help others. He's a good man.'

Hotaka had to agree. His grandfather was always doing something for someone. He never thought about himself.

'We all need to follow his lead, you know, now more than ever. It's in terrible times like this that we should reach out and help one another. Most of all we must help those lost in darkness to find at least *some* light, even if it's only a flicker.' He slapped his hand on Hotaka's shoulder. 'Actions. Always do what is right.'

The abbot bade Hotaka farewell and crossed to the bell house, climbing its steps; it was time to ring the bonsho. At the bell he bowed three times, as he would to the Buddha. Then he pulled back the shu-moku, the log, and let it strike the bell. The sound was clear and strong, gradually changing to a deep hum that hung in the air like mist. Hotaka's grandfather had once told him that if you listen properly to a bonsho's call, it never completely fades but stays in you forever. With that thought, Hotaka walked away feeling a little calmer.

He passed his school, deciding not to go through the gate. He guessed that quite a few students must have been taken by the wave – those who hadn't gone to the puppet theatre – for there were many parents milling around. Seeing the grief on their faces would be too difficult to bear. And what if Takeshi's parents were there? What would he say to them? What *could* he say?

So he kept moving and before long came to the gym Mr Grumpy had spoken of, the one that had been transformed into a morgue. People and vehicles were passing in and out, a constant flow of sorrow. As he reached the main gate a truck turned in laden with large black plastic bags, a pungent odour trailing behind. The smell of death, Hotaka decided with a shudder, and cupped his hand over his nostrils. A man passed by with a body in a barrow. Behind the gym three portable incinerators were all pumping smoke. Cremations, Hotaka realised with horror. Bodies were being burnt here. Many of them. Once more a great weight of sadness descended upon him.

He wanted to run away, but noticed a boy sitting on the steps of the gym. His head was buried in his hands, so his face wasn't visible, but something familiar about him made Hotaka move closer. The boy was thin and gangly, his hair a tangled mess, his clothes crumpled and ill-fitting. A pair of black thick-lensed spectacles lay on the step beside him. Hotaka knew those specs.

'Osamu?' he said. 'Is that you?'

The boy lifted his head and squinted up, eyes red and puffy.

'Hotaka.' His voice was husky. 'What are you doing here?'

34

'Nothing. I was just passing. And you?' Hotaka asked with a sense of foreboding. 'What about you?'

Osamu immediately looked away – at the people, at the ground, anywhere rather than at Hotaka. He grabbed his spectacles and made a fumbling attempt to clean them, dropping them instead. Hotaka picked them up.

Osamu was in Hotaka's class. They'd been in the same class as each other since starting school. But they'd never been friends; they were too different for that. Osamu was the school geek, a tech head, a bookworm, the whiz kid who wore specs that were like magnifying glasses and who could code before he even went to school. Hotaka was into sport: baseball, soccer, sailing, running, anything physical. They had nothing in common, and in fact Hotaka couldn't remember the last time they'd actually spoken to each other.

'Here,' he said, holding out the spectacles. Osamu took them without looking up, muttering his thanks. He then stared at them intently, his hands shaking. Hotaka sat down next to Osamu. 'What is it?' he asked quietly. 'What's the matter?'

It took Osamu ages to answer, as if the words refused to come out.

'My parents are dead.'

Hotaka gasped. He'd guessed that Osamu must have lost someone important, but he never imagined this. Both parents dead? Unthinkable. Unimaginable. He struggled for something to say.

'Are you sure?' he blurted out, immediately regretting it.

Osamu turned and glared at him. 'What do you think?' he shouted. 'I've seen them, in there, in body bags. I can still see them. I'll see them for the rest of my life! Cold and grey and…and *dead*!'

The last word came out as a long, lonely howl, and Osamu sobbed uncontrollably.

Hotaka could see and hear the boy's pain, and wanted to comfort him but didn't know how. 'I'm sorry,' he cried. 'That was stupid of me. I really am so sorry.'

He held Osamu tightly, waiting for the sobbing to ebb. When it eventually did, the boy sat back.

'I'm sorry, too,' he said. 'For shouting at you. I know you didn't mean to be stupid.'

'That's all right, bud,' Hotaka replied. 'It's just the way I am. Stupid. Comes naturally.'

Osamu laughed weakly and the boys sat in silence.

'What will you do?' Hotaka asked after a while.

'No idea. I only know that I don't want to go home. I'd be on my own.'

'Isn't there anybody in Omori-wan who—?'

'No,' Osamu said. 'All I have is my grandmother in Tokyo. The police have contacted her but she can't be here until next week. I'd be all alone in that big house, and I don't think I could stand it. I spent all last night there alone, waiting for my parents, when they would already have been…dead. I couldn't go back there tonight. I'd feel them everywhere, in every room.'

'Then you'll just have to stay at my house.'

Osamu's face brightened. 'Do you mean it?'

'Of course I do.' Hotaka stood and held out his hand. 'Hurry up, before I change my mind.'

# Seven

**'Stay as long as you want.'**

Hotaka's mother knelt beside Osamu. She had been hugging him and weeping with him. Now she was holding his hands, gently stroking them. 'Consider yourself one of the family,' Hotaka's mother added.

'Yamato-san, arigatō gozaimasu, thank you very much. I cannot tell you how much that means. But you won't have to put up with me for long, I promise; my grandmother will be here within the week; I'm sure she will.'

'No need for that, Osamu. Whenever she gets here. I mean it!' Hotaka's mother rose, crossing to the furu, a small black metal brazier that heated the room. 'Now let's get something warm and nourishing into you boys.'

They were in a small room just off the central courtyard of Hotaka's house. His mother called it the chashitsu, the tea room, but it was used for all sorts of things in winter, being cosy and easy to heat. A large earthen pot sat on the brazier. Mrs Yamato lifted the lid, took a ladle and prepared two bowls of steaming miso soup thick with delicious noodles.

'I assume you're hungry,' she said to Osamu, placing a bowl in front of him on the low table. He nodded eagerly. 'And you must be starving, Hotaka,' she added. 'I know for a fact that you didn't have breakfast before you sneaked out and left me fretting all day. The whole mobile network was down so I didn't know what to think.' She frowned as she handed him his bowl. 'You had me worried sick!'

'I am sorry, Okāsan, I really am. But there was something I *had* to do.'

His mother sighed. 'I understand. I too had some...' She didn't finish, shaking her head instead. 'What a terrible thing this is that has come upon us.' She placed the lid back on the crock.

Hotaka detected a note of strain in his mother's voice. Something was distressing her, something more than his disappearance all day, he felt sure. It was bigger than that, and he could see it in her face as well. Was it to do with Uncle Yori? Had she heard something? Hotaka wanted to ask, though not in front of Osamu. Later, he decided.

Just then his mother suddenly clapped her hands. 'Which reminds me,' she said, regaining her composure. 'You won't be the only one staying with us, Osamu. We're taking in some guests.'

'Guests?' Hotaka said. 'Who?'

'Anyone who has lost their home. The government is sending portable huts and units, but they'll be days, probably weeks away. It will take months to set those up and house everyone. In the meantime it's up to people like us, who have homes, to look after those who don't. Simple as that. I've been to all the homes on this side of Omori-wan, and most have agreed to take in people.'

'How many are we taking?'

'I've calculated we could handle maybe fourteen, but we'll go for ten to begin and work upwards if we can.'

'Wow! That's a lot of people, Okāsan. We'll be crowded.'

'I know. It won't be easy, Hotaka. It'll be a shock after just having you, me and Jīchan. We'll be cramped, but it's our duty to those less fortunate. I'm sure you understand.'

'Of course.'

His mother smiled and picked up the soup ladle again. 'I suggest you boys make the most of your relative privacy this evening. It could be the last quiet night for a while.' She held up the ladle. 'More soup?'

They both nodded. She filled their bowls.

'And when you finish, Osamu,' she added, 'there's a hot bath. Hotaka will show you what's what.'

'Yamato-san, arigatō gozaimasu,' Osamu replied. 'You are so kind.'

As his mother left the room, Hotaka noticed that shadow of concern pass across her face again, and decided to discover what the problem was once he'd looked after Osamu.

Hotaka found his mother in the kitchen, staring into the sink.

'What is it, Okāsan?' She turned to him and he could see she'd been crying. 'Bad news?'

'No, my son. I'm just – oh, I don't know – overwhelmed by all the tragedy around us.'

She took a deep breath.

'My heart weeps for Osamu, and yet he's just one of many, *many* people. I helped in town for much of the day, handing out food, clothes, blankets, trying to comfort people who have lost everything. And I mean *everything*, Hotaka. We're so lucky, my son. We've lost nothing.' She closed her eyes for a moment. 'And seeing so much loss and grief made me realise how important your grandfather and uncle are. They're the only family we have. They're everything to us.'

She didn't mention his father, but then he wouldn't have expected her to. Hotaka's parents had formally separated a year ago, although his father had been often absent for several years. He now lived in Tokyo, with his business and his young mistress. The absence of a proper father figure hurt Hotaka deeply, but luckily his grandfather and uncle had stepped into the role. They were precious to him; he couldn't imagine life without them.

'And not having them here – right here with us now I mean – makes me so worried, so frightened.'

'No, Okāsan, you must not think that way.'

'I know it's silly, but I can't help worrying.'

'They're both fine.'

'Really? Both? I know Jīchan is safe up in the hills with Rho-san. But what of Uncle Yori?'

'I meant to tell you I saw his boat clear the wave. I'm certain of it!'

40

His mother nodded. 'Is that so, Hotaka? I know there have been reports of boats at sea, unable to return but safe nonetheless.'

'Exactly, and he's one of those for sure; you can bet on it. Uncle Yori is a survivor.'

'That's true, I suppose.'

'He's out there, Okāsan, floating around, waiting for his chance to come back, believe me.'

Hotaka's mother held up her hands. 'Okay, my son. I believe you.' She stepped away from the sink. 'Mind you, I still wish Jīchan was here with us. I miss his soft voice, his calm reassurance. He has always been such a rock for me.'

'For me, too, Okāsan.'

'I actually tried calling Rho-san last night, and this morning. But of course all the networks were down and I couldn't get through. I tried again around lunchtime today; still no luck. I'd just like to hear Jīchan's voice, that's all.'

'I know. I'd like it, too, more than anything. But he will be with us as soon as the roads are cleared. He will!' Hotaka reached out and took his mother's hand.

'You're right, of course,' his mother replied, smiling weakly. She straightened herself. 'I suppose I should really get on and prepare a couple of rooms. Our first guests will be arriving in the morning. There's even a chance some may come this evening.'

'Good idea,' Hotaka said. 'I'll help you.'

'So will I.' Osamu stood at the kitchen door, fresh from his bath.

# Eight

**Several guests did arrive later** that night. Soon after Hotaka's mother and the boys had set up some rooms, Abbot Etsudo brought two families and three old people; all had lost their homes. He also brought a pile of mattresses, sheets, blankets and towels, as well as bags of second-hand clothes; most people had only what was on their backs. He had boxes of food, too – mainly rice, noodles and tins – promising to return with more in a few days.

'No need for all that,' Hotaka's mother insisted. 'We will feed and provide bedding for our guests.'

The abbot bowed. 'That is most generous of you, Yamato-san.'

'Not at all, Jūshoku-san. It's the least we can do.'

After the abbot left, Hotaka and Osamu helped feed the guests and settle them in. They all wanted to talk – needed to talk – of what had happened to them, of what they'd seen and heard, and how they felt. Their loss was great, their grief deep; the talking seemed to ease their pain a little.

It was after ten by the time they were ready for bed. Hotaka could see that his mother was exhausted, so he took charge, escorting each group of guests in turn to their rooms. Then he made sure Osamu was settled before eventually returning to his mother to say goodnight.

She was standing in the hall outside her bedroom, swaying slightly as if unsure on her feet, one hand on the wall to support herself. Hotaka rushed straight to her side.

'Okāsan! What's the matter?'

Her face was pale, her body trembling. But she steadied herself and raised her other hand, clutching her phone. 'That was Rho-san. He was breaking up all the time, and I lost him eventually, the network down again. But I heard enough.'

'What? What did you hear?'

'Jīchan left yesterday.'

'To come home?'

'Yes. On the bus.'

'What bus? What time?'

'Rho-san wasn't absolutely sure. He thought Jīchan caught the midday bus.'

'But that means he could have, no, *would* have arrived just about when the earthquake hit.'

'I know. That's if Rho-san is right.'

'What's wrong with him?' Hotaka shouted. 'Why doesn't he know what bus?'

'Don't be angry with Rho-san. Jīchan says his old friend is more forgetful every day, and I must say he sounded awfully vague on the phone.'

'But it makes all the difference in the world, Okāsan!'

'I know it does. If Jīchan caught a later bus he's probably just stuck somewhere. There would have been no way in or out of Omori-wan yesterday *after* the quake and tsunami, and I bet the roads are still in a dreadful mess.'

'But if he caught the midday bus—'

'No, my son.' His mother cut him short, pressing her fingers against his lips. 'Don't say it. Just because we don't know for certain doesn't mean we must think the worst.'

Hotaka and his mother stared at each other in silence. Eventually she pulled him close and hugged him hard.

'Tomorrow,' she whispered. 'We'll find out all we can first thing tomorrow.'

'But—'

'Hush, my son. It's how you told me to think about Uncle Yori: wait until we know for sure. Tomorrow.'

Hotaka allowed himself to sink into his mother, letting her calm ease his fears. 'Of course, Okāsan.'

Hotaka collapsed onto his futon, drained and distraught, his mind swimming in a sea of emotion. So many doubts and fears and visions swirling around him. Takeshi, Grandpa, Uncle Yori, they were all there in his thoughts, looming large, surrounded by the welter of terrible things he'd seen that day, and the day before.

And then there was Osamu. He was on the other side of the room, lying on his back, his silhouette just visible, his breathing slow and even. Hotaka tried to imagine the agonies his new friend must be suffering, the thoughts coursing through his mind, the nightmares brewing, but he found it too distressing. At least Osamu was asleep,

Hotaka was pleased to see, and rolled on his side with a mind to do the same.

Hotaka woke suddenly the next morning, well before sunrise. He sat up at once, eyes wide open, jolted from his sleep.

He dressed quickly and quietly. Osamu was sound asleep, one foot and a clump of wild hair visible. No one else was up yet as Hotaka sneaked down the hall and out into the crisp morning. To his left, the road past his house went over the top of Monk Head Hill and then curved back down into Omori-wan. On his right, the road went along the top of a ridge that led to the northern headland of Omori Bay.

Hotaka turned right and set off briskly. The morning was free of mist and fog, the air remarkably clear, allowing glimpses of the Pacific Ocean through the trees on his left. Omori-wan and the bay were on his other side but not visible from the road.

He came to a narrow path on his left, and his spirits immediately lifted. At least he now knew *where* he was going: Eagle Cliff, that special place where he and Takeshi came so many times, the spot where they threw themselves into the sea, each in their own way.

Hotaka turned down the path and followed it until it emerged from the trees. There he paused and stared across a clearing. About twenty metres away was that drop into the sea. He breathed in and slowly crossed the clearing, his heart beating faster with each step. Soon he was standing at the very edge of Eagle Cliff.

The sun was still below the horizon, although its golden-red glow was growing with every second. Hotaka gazed north and south as far as he could see up and down the coast. He couldn't help wondering how other places had fared in the earthquake and tsunami, big centres like Kesennuma, Rikuzentakata and Kamaishi. Abbot Etsudo and the guests had talked of devastation along hundreds of kilometres of the Tōhoku coast.

All that destruction and death! Hotaka turned his eyes angrily on the ocean. That's where it came from, he thought. That's where the monster lay, the thing that had washed his world away, somewhere out there. Yet it was almost impossible to imagine such violence and chaos now, for there was barely a ripple to be seen that morning. The ocean was calm and still, as if waiting for the sun to wake and warm its skin.

Suddenly the sun appeared, a mere glint of light but surprisingly bright. And in that brightness it dawned on Hotaka – the reason for his being there, in that particular place, at that particular time. He was there for the three people uppermost in his mind: Uncle Yori, Grandpa, and Takeshi. This place held a special bond through him to each of them.

It was from here that he'd often seen Uncle Yori's bright blue and white trawler heading out to sea or returning with a catch. He peered out now, scanning the horizon, searching for any sign of his uncle's boat, wishing and hoping. Nothing, and yet he was certain that all was fine with the big fisherman.

He then pulled right back and let his gaze drop to a

tiny beach some way along from the bottom of the cliff. He called it Grandpa's Beach. His grandfather had often taken him there, sailing in his little sabani all the way from Omori Bay out into the sea and north. Grandpa always brought a picnic, and sat on the beach while Hotaka swam among the rocks.

'Where are you, Jīchan?' he whispered to the little beach. 'Please be okay. Please!'

And then there was the very deep body of water directly below Hotaka at the base of the cliff. That was where Takeshi always dived. He would sprint across the clearing and spring from the cliff, slicing through the air. His slim spearlike body would pierce the emerald water, his happy face bursting the surface a moment later, followed by that infectious laugh of his. And the yelling, of course. Always the yelling.

'Come on, Hotaka, jump. Hurry up, I'm waiting. Jump!'

There wasn't any yelling now, though. No laughing, either. No splash to be heard. No emerald sparkling water, the sea below a cold steely grey, everything as still as a grave.

Hotaka fell to his knees, cries echoing in his head – cries of anguish, over and over.

*Takeshi.*
*Where are you, my friend?*
*Uncle Yori.*
*Jīchan.*
*I need you all. Where are you?*

2014

*I was given a book of the names of the dead so I would be sure to spell them correctly in both Kanji and English. In return I made a book of the living and gave it back to them, of those who faced the Wave and died, of those who learned to live.*

*Facing the Wave: A Journey in the Wake of the Tsunami,*
Gretel Ehrlich

# Nine

**It is our duty to remember.** *But we must also look forward.*

Hotaka stares at his words. They are from an essay he wrote about the 3/11 tsunami. Last year there was a competition and schools from all over the area entered. His essay won and he was asked to read it aloud at that year's memorial ceremony in Rikuzentakata.

People cried as he read. They stood and clapped when he finished, and after the ceremony many thanked him. Some said his words spoke to them personally. Others could only shake his hand in silence and bow; he could feel their emotion. In that moment Hotaka realised the importance of hope in people's lives. So when Miss Abe came to him bubbling excitedly about her idea, he was glad to listen.

Miss Abe had retrained to become a junior high school teacher. After the 3/11 tsunami she found it impossible to return to the elementary school; it held too many bad personal memories from the tsunami. So she took time off to gain higher qualifications. Much to Hotaka's delight she became his class teacher on returning to her teaching career last year. He is glad of that. Young and alive, Miss Abe's eyes shine and her laugh is infectious; she makes school worthwhile.

'I've had a brainwave,' she told him the day after he gave his speech in Rikuzentakata. 'It's obvious what we have to do.'

Hotaka stared blankly. 'Do, Abe-sensei? We?'

'Yes, we. You, me, all of us, the school.' She spread her arms wide. 'Get this. Next year the school holds a 3/11 memorial ceremony that's a celebration of Tōhoku culture – singing, dancing, mysticism, music, everything. Let's showcase our richness, all those things we should be remembering, and kick out the shadows. It's time we moved on. Forward!'

Hotaka loved the idea.

'Of course we'll have to persuade Principal Hashimoto and others.' She rolled her eyes. 'But I think I can manage it.' She gave Hotaka the sweetest of smiles, leaving him in no doubt that she'd manage it. 'Most of all, though, I'll need your help to make it happen. Say yes?' She flashed that smile again.

'I'd be honoured, Abe-sensei,' Hotaka replied. 'Arigatō gozaimasu – thank you for asking me.'

She shook his hand vigorously. 'No. I should be thanking *you*: for saying yes and for giving me the idea in the first place. After your reading yesterday, I knew you'd be perfect.' She stood back, her eyes sparkling more than ever. 'There'll be a lot to do, you know, but we'll have the whole year to do it in. Let's give them something they'll never forget.'

Hotaka puts down the essay, picks up a sheet of paper and crosses to his bedroom window. It's about an hour until sunrise, the sky smudged with muted pastels. He glances at the paper – the program for the school's Memorial Concert – and smiles.

Principal Hashimoto and the School Board loved Miss Abe's idea. So with help from some teachers and students – especially Hotaka – she has spent much of the year lining up events and performers. She sweet-talked and cajoled a whole range of people to be part of the show, creating an exciting program for the Omori-wan Junior High School Memorial Concert.

Now with about a fortnight before the concert, Hotaka's job is to confirm that the main presenters are all fully prepared and happy with their place in the program. He's already contacted a few, like Abbot Etsudo, but there are still plenty to get in touch with: the Puppet People; the old geisha; the poets; and of course the Shaman Lady. Hotaka is visiting her this morning. He hopes she'll remember.

There's a soft knock at his door, and his mother pokes her head into the room.

'Can't sleep?' she asks.

He shrugs. 'We're a good pair, aren't we, Okāsan? I suppose you have something on today?'

'Always busy,' she replies. 'Yes, an important luncheon.'

Since 3/11 Hotaka's mother has devoted herself to fundraising for the needy throughout the Tōhoku region. On the very first day after the tsunami she opened her

53

house to as many as she could fit – sixteen at one stage – housing and feeding them for well over a month until relief accommodation was organised. She's been active in the role ever since, often to the point of exhaustion. Omori-wan missed out on much of the foreign aid that flowed into the region, leaving the little town dependent on government aid and the selfless work of people like Hotaka's mother.

'What's the luncheon in aid of?' Hotaka asks.

'A shelter for the truly desperate,' she replies. 'There are still many forgotten people in the area. The shelter will be somewhere they can go and know there'll be help. We've collected two-thirds of the funds. This luncheon should guarantee the rest.'

As she speaks, the sun peeps over the horizon, its soft rays highlighting the side of her face. Hotaka can't help noticing her features – high forehead, petite nose, strong jaw – struck by what a proud woman she is. She turns to him.

'And you, my son?'

'I'm visiting the Shaman Lady first thing this morning.'

'Fox Woman? How come?'

'She's in the Memorial Concert.'

'Wow! She's nuts, you know?'

'Maybe, but Abe-sensei wants her in the show because she represents the power of our Tōhoku myths and legends better than anyone.'

'True, and she is a respected figure among the older people. Your Memorial Concert sounds good. Are you seeing Fox Woman on your own?'

'No. Osamu's coming, if he manages to wake up.'

'How is Osamu? I haven't seen him in weeks.'

'He's okay. He's really too full on and in your face these days, but he's okay.'

'Glad to hear it. I'll never forget what a broken little boy he was after the wave. You were such a good friend to him in that early difficult time. I think that's what got him through. That plus his grandmother, of course, who looks after him and feeds him so well.'

Hotaka nods. He remembers that time just after the tsunami, and how hard it was for Osamu. But the weird geeky guy gradually grew on Hotaka. He now considers Osamu his best friend. Along with Sakura, that is.

'Sakura's coming too.'

'Really?' His mother raises her eyebrows. 'I like that girl. She's smart.'

Hotaka smiles. Smart? What an understatement. He recalls the first time he met Sakura. She simply turned up at school one day about a year ago, a refugee from who knows where. There was nothing unusual in that; the social dislocation after 3/11 had strewn people throughout the Tōhoku region and beyond. She was alone, too, no adult in tow. That wasn't unusual either. But her small solitary figure made her seem vulnerable.

Maybe that's why Hotaka and Osamu walked up and spoke to her. They soon discovered she was in fact far from vulnerable. That very first morning she corrected Mr Tamura in Maths. In after-school activities she beat the school chess champ, and she even sorted a coding problem for Osamu. The geek was smitten – and Hotaka was definitely interested.

'Oh well, you'll have company,' his mother continues. 'Should be fun.'

Hotaka shakes his head. 'Not necessarily. Those two can be tough work.'

'How do you mean?'

'At each other's throats.'

'But I thought they were friends. You three spend a lot of time together.'

'Oh yeah, they're friends. You just wouldn't know it sometimes. They argue heaps, always winding each other up. It gets hard to take after a while.'

His mother laughs. 'They sound like great company.' She hugs him. 'Have fun.'

'You, too, Okāsan.'

# Ten

**Hotaka sits in a heavy** late winter fog, under an ancient oak tree where monks of old paused on their travels. It's at the four-way intersection on top of Monk Head Hill. He's waiting for Osamu and Sakura to come on the road up from Omori-wan. They'll then head west a couple of kilometres to the Shaman Lady's cottage. As expected, his friends are late; Osamu has no idea of time.

Hotaka breathes in the early morning air and catches the unpleasant smell of diesel. He can't see the town for the fog, but he can hear it. The racket of reconstruction has already started for the day, noises that have defined his town for three years now. Every day the same rumble rises from the valley – the relentless grind and growl of bulldozers, trucks, tractors, graders and excavators. It's hard enough to endure where he lives, but must be unbearable for those in the town itself.

'This is ridiculous. I could be still in bed!'

Hotaka knows the voice at once. It's Osamu.

'Well go back to bed. We'll all be happy then.'

And that's Sakura. Hotaka peers into the fog.

His friends emerge from the mist, Sakura stepping out at a good pace, Osamu metres behind, puffing as he pushes his bike. Hotaka nearly calls out, but holds back, amused at what a funny pair they make.

Osamu is long and thin like a string bean; he's shot up in the last two years. Uncoordinated and gangly, with dishevelled hair, huge dark-rimmed specs and the dress-sense of a brick, he's every inch the uber-geek. By contrast, Sakura is tiny, a good two heads shorter. She's dressed totally in black, and rugged up against the cold. As she approaches, she throws back her hood, revealing a crop of spiky blonde hair with flaming red tips. The first time Hotaka met Sakura her hair was *all* red, fluoro red; she looked like a walking flare. At the time he thought she might be an attention-seeker. He soon changed his mind; it was her way of warning: Handle with Care!

'Seriously though,' Osamu complains, 'what kind of idiot gets up at a quarter to sunrise and battles a miserable fog just to visit some crazy lady, when they could be tucked up in bed?'

'Me,' Hotaka calls, grabbing his bike and joining them. 'I'm that kind of idiot. And it looks like you two are as well.'

'You can say that again,' Osamu mutters, leaning on his bike for a spell.

'Don't bother stopping,' Hotaka says, hopping onto his bike. 'We're late already.' He beckons to Sakura. 'Come on, up you get.' She climbs on behind and he pedals off.

'Oh great,' Osamu groans. 'Just great.'

The Shaman Lady is waiting at her cottage door when they arrive. She bustles Sakura and Osamu in, but stops Hotaka as he passes.

'One moment, wakaino, young man,' she hisses, grabbing his arm with a surprisingly powerful grip. She peers hard at him. 'Strange. Very strange.'

'Is something wrong, obaba, wise old woman?' Hotaka asks.

'I could have sworn…' She shakes her head and pushes him inside, muttering: 'All is ready, all is ready.'

The air in the cottage is stale and musty, heavy with smoke and incense. It's dark and cramped in there too, the ceiling so low that Osamu has to stoop. Once their eyes adjust, the teenagers soon see that the room is crowded with old people squatting and kneeling. The young ones keep back, close to the door.

The Shaman Lady shuffles past to the middle of the room and lights a candle. The crowd immediately begins humming. The hum gradually grows louder. When it reaches a deep throb, the old woman thrusts her hands in the air, and the hum stops.

'Namazu,' she hisses. 'We know it is you!'

She shakes a bony finger at the figures squatting on the earthen floor, their wide-eyed faces flickering in the candlelight.

'Namazu! That is who!' She growls now. 'Shaker of the Earth, harbinger of death and destruction, misery and misfortune.'

Heads nod, agreement grunts around the room.

'Ever since time began you have lurked in the mud at the bottom of the sea, waiting to escape the god Kashima, to wriggle free and thrash your tail, making the earth quake and break.'

She takes a deep breath, slowly straightening her arthritic body.

'Namazu! *You* are to blame,' she wails, raising her withered arms, swaying in a trance-like dance. '*You* whipped up the wave that washed our world away!'

She chants in a high-pitched howl, claw-like hands lashing at the air.

'*Washed our world away!*'

The squatting figures rise, bent and bowed. They shuffle forward and surround the shaman, swaying and chanting.

'*Washed our world away!*'

The old people are wailing and weeping as Hotaka and his friends watch from the side of the room.

'*Washed our world away.*'

'Oh my god,' Sakura whispers. 'I know you warned me, Hotaka, but…' She shrugs. 'I don't know what to say.'

He nods. 'Maybe that's because there's nothing we can say. Us, I mean. Our generation.'

'Crap!' Osamu snaps. 'I could say heaps – like crazy, weird, nuts, cuckoo welcome to the fruit-cake club.' He raises his voice to match the wailing. 'What a load of loonies!'

'Osamu!' Hotaka hisses. 'Have some respect.'

'Respect? I'll have fresh air, thanks.' Osamu turns and

walks off, calling over his shoulder. 'I knew I shouldn't have come. Freakin' freak show.'

'Wait, Osamu.'

'Let him go,' Sakura says. 'He's just being his usual stupid self.'

It's not that simple, Hotaka wants to tell Sakura. Osamu's *stupid self*, as she calls it, can sometimes be a front for his frightened self, the scared little boy who still wakes to nightmare visions of his parents in body bags. She knows nothing of Osamu's deep depression for almost a year after the tsunami. It was only Hotaka's loyalty that stopped him ending his life. But Sakura knows nothing of this either. Then again why would she? It's all part of Osamu's hidden self.

'I don't know why you brought him,' Sakura adds.

'I brought him because we all should see this. *Us.* Like Abe-sensei says: it connects us to a past we need to remember.'

Sakura doesn't reply, but allows her hand to brush briefly against his, and they watch the ritual in silence.

Pain fills the room like a fog. Hotaka knows how deeply the tsunami hurt these old ones. Despite the years, the horror is still with them, wounds that will never heal. The wave swallowed their friends. Many here wish they'd been swallowed as well. So little of their past remains, and no future waits to welcome them.

Their grief tears at his heart. But he also cannot get Osamu out of his head. Maybe it wasn't such a good idea to bring him. What if his friend's rant about the Fox Woman was more than it seemed? What if it wasn't the myth and make-believe that upset Osamu, but all the emotion in that room, all the memories threatening to drown him? Maybe he didn't storm out in anger, but was chased out by his own fear.

'Kuso, damn!' Hotaka curses, annoyed with himself.

'What is it?' Sakura asks.

'Maybe we should go,' he whispers. 'I'm sure the Shaman Lady will understand.'

They edge backwards to the low doorway, keeping their faces turned to the old people as a sign of respect. When they reach the door, Sakura opens it, bows and backs out of the room. Hotaka pauses a moment, then does the same.

But before he closes the door his gaze is caught by the Shaman Lady. For an instant he feels her eyes reach right into his soul.

He knows what she's seen.

# Eleven

**As Hotaka and Sakura pull** on their coats and beanies, they see Osamu waiting by the gate out of the Shaman Lady's place. Hotaka calls and they head towards him. But the cottage door creaks open and the old woman emerges.

'Wakaino,' she calls, and scurries across to him like a gnarled gnome. 'Wait.'

'You go ahead,' Hotaka says to Sakura. 'I'll catch up. And be nice to Osamu, eh?'

She frowns. 'What did you say?'

'Doesn't matter,' he replies and turns to the Shaman Lady.

'What is it, obaba? If our friend has offended you, gomen nasai, I am truly sorry! He meant no offence. He was unwell and needed fresh air.'

'It is for you I worry,' the woman insists. 'I must see for myself.' She latches onto his arm, her sharp eyes scanning his body. 'When you arrived I thought I saw something on your back. When I looked again it was not there. Perhaps I was imagining things, but I *must* be sure.'

'It's nothing, really.'

'Silence!'

He knows exactly what the old woman is looking for, but doesn't want her prying. He begins to pull away and she tightens her grip.

'There is something,' she whispers. 'I cannot see it, but I can *sense* it. It is well hidden, almost part of you.' Her eyes sear into him. 'A presence without form.'

'You must be imagining things,' Hotaka stammers.

'Stay still,' she snaps. 'A spirit, yes! A ghost of sorts.'

'An evil spirit?' Hotaka asks. But he already knows the answer.

'Certainly not! This one is gentle. And it *was* happy once.' She concentrates. 'But it is lost, untethered. Yes, an unclaimed spirit searching for peace.'

Hotaka doesn't want this, but the woman won't let go. She points a bony finger at him.

'I think you know what I'm talking about.' She raises her eyebrows. 'You and this spirit have been together for some time. Mmmm?'

Hotaka shakes his head. 'I've no idea what you mean.'

'Yes, you do.' She brings her face right up to his. 'Understand this. There comes a time when we must let go of those who have been precious to us in life. It does none of us any good to hold on for too long. We only imprison each other that way.' The old woman's eyes reach right into him.

'I understand, obaba.'

'I hope so. For as hard as it might be to let go, it is for the best.' She relaxes her grip and pats his arm gently. 'Off with you now. I'll see you at the concert.'

'Oh yes, of course.' Hotaka had completely forgotten about that, his reason for visiting the old woman. 'Abe-sensei will be pleased.' He bows. 'Arigatō gozaimasu.'

'You take care, wakaino. Take *special* care.'

The Shaman Lady shuffles back to the cottage. Hotaka breathes a huge sigh of relief and pedals off.

When Hotaka catches up to his friends, he's glad to see that Osamu seems fine. They're arguing, as expected, but there's no anger in Osamu's tone. In fact Sakura sounds like the angry bird. They're too engrossed to notice Hotaka, so he coasts quietly behind them, listening in.

'You're wrong,' Osamu declares. 'She was spewing up mumbo jumbo.'

'Maybe, but she had her audience captivated.'

'Those old peasants? Get real. How hard could that be? They were as crazy as her.'

'I thought she was awesome.'

'Awesome? Awful, you mean. She was peddling lies.'

'What do you mean?'

'News flash: the 3/11 disaster was not caused by Namazu, or by any other creature, demon or denizen of the freakin' deep.'

'Dude! We all know that.'

'No, *dude*, those old people don't. That witch was pumping them full of lies.'

'Come on!' Sakura shouts. 'It's an explanation to help them make sense of—'

'Oh, great explanation.' Osamu sniggers. 'It's a fairy-tale, a total con. And that got me really angry in there, because far from making sense of anything, it makes *nonsense of everything* and explains nothing. Hear me? Zilch, zip, zero, nix, *not a single thing*!'

'Of course it's nonsense. But it's part of our culture.'

'So that makes it all right, does it? Sorry, but calling something part of our culture doesn't mean we have to accept it, or that it's even any good.'

'I know that. But all those myths and legends are kind of what makes us who we are.'

'Speak for yourself. That stuff is not part of who I am. No way!'

'I don't mean personally. It's part of our heritage, our national makeup, and it works for those people.'

'More fool them, then. That stuff might've been cool hundreds of years ago, but the world has moved on. We know what caused the tsunami. It's called an earthquake! That's spelt—'

'Shut it!' Sakura flares. 'You're missing the point, you idiot!' She spins around to face Osamu, and sees Hotaka. 'I'm right, aren't I? He's just being a dumb-arse, isn't he?'

Hotaka laughs. 'He's actually just winding you up.'

'Me?' Osamu plays innocent. 'Wind her up? Never.'

Sakura glares at Osamu, then spins round and marches off.

Osamu frowns at Hotaka. 'I was having fun.'

'I could see that, you idiot. Come on, we can't let her go off in a huff.'

They soon reach the edge of the hill that overlooks

Omori-wan from the west. The fog has lifted enough to see the town. Sakura is waiting, hands on hips.

'Now *that* is what you should be angry about,' she tells Osamu. 'Forget the shaman. *That* should make your blood boil.'

'What?' Osamu screws up his face.

'That!' Sakura snaps, sweeping her arms over the view of the town. 'Down there.'

'Sorry, you've lost me.'

Osamu is doing it again – winding up Sakura. It annoys Hotaka this time; his friend is being silly when he shouldn't be. That's the trouble with Osamu: he never knows when to pull back, when a joke is no longer a joke. He doesn't have an off-switch.

He knows how important Omori-wan is to Sakura. She may not be from the town, but she's taken it on as her own. Hotaka once showed her some photographs of how beautiful the place was before the tsunami, and she wept. Ever since then she's been passionate about what's happening to Omori-wan in the name of so-called reconstruction; what's being done and what isn't.

'Just open your eyes, will you?' she shouts at Osamu. 'See the nightmare down there. That's not a town – it's a lot of concrete, dirt, gravel and bitumen smattered with tiny temporary dwellings. People don't live there, they exist at best. And the powers that be call it a reconstruction program? Ha! I call it a big lie, a huge con, loads of money for Mayor Nakano and Co, and nothing for anyone else. In the three years since the tsunami, nothing has been spent on housing for people. But what's the mayor's next big project? A seawall! – a monstrous structure that will cost a fortune. That's criminal!'

'Dude,' Osamu says, 'that's big business.' He holds up both hands, rubbing his thumbs and fingers together. 'That's how things are done. Part of our culture, if you like.'

'But no one says anything. No one even makes a noise. We're being ripped off, but we take it lying down, like frightened mice.'

'That's part of our culture too. We bow to authority in Japan. We do as we're told. Always have. Always will.'

'Oh, I see.' Sakura has a glint in her eye. She steps right up to Osamu. 'So that makes it okay, does it? Sorry, kid, but a little way back, you told me that – and I quote – calling something part of our culture doesn't mean we have to accept it, or that it's even good!'

Osamu's face reddens. 'Aw now, that's different,' he blusters.

'It sure is different. Back there was just you being your usual silly self. This is serious.' Sakura points to Omori-wan. 'You only have to look down there to see how serious.'

Hotaka howls with laughter. 'Checkmate, bud. She got you. Admit it.'

Sakura grins up at Osamu. 'Well?'

He shrugs. 'Yeah, okay, you win, I guess. One all… for today.'

Sakura laughs, then springs forward and snatches Osamu's bike from under his nose. Before he can do anything, she leaps on and pedals off down the hill to Omori-wan.

'Thanks, loser,' she shouts. 'See you at school.'

Osamu runs after her, but she's too fast. When he turns around, Hotaka is still laughing.

'Very funny!' Osamu mutters. 'Now I'll be late for my Advanced Programming workshop.' He kicks at the ground. 'And that is serious.'

He does look genuinely upset, so Hotaka takes pity on him. 'Don't cry,' he replies. 'You can have my bike.'

'You sure?'

'Yeah. I've got a free period first up. I'll be reporting to Abe-sensei about out visit to the Shaman Lady.' Hotaka doesn't add that he feels like being alone for a bit.

'Thanks, bud,' Osamu says as he takes the bike. 'I owe you one.'

'You do indeed.'

# Twelve

**Hotaka is pleased to be alone.** He loves Osamu and Sakura, but sometimes their company is like being in a pressure cooker. It's good to have time-out from them now and then. Time to think.

He looks over the town, Sakura's comments in his head. They have unsettled him, and he needs to think things through a bit.

Of course she's right about the housing problem, and how ugly and soulless the town is. Dirt, gravel, bitumen and concrete – that's Omori-wan. The harbour has been repaired, with a new marina, a wide road and new buildings along the front. But the marina is badly built, a rushed job of poor craftsmanship. The road is bitumen rather than cobblestones, and the buildings are concrete blocks, functional but charmless. And all the tiny temporary housing units are simply hideous.

One building does stand out – the Town Hall. Money has been lavished on it, especially the upper level which houses Mayor Nakano's office, a palace of glass and concrete. They say an entertainment facility is planned for that level, too, with bars, a restaurant and maybe even gambling. So Sakura is probably right about the corruption as well.

What of the seawall, though? Is she right about that? Hotaka wonders.

He gazes past the harbour to the far side of the marina, where work has begun on the wall. Only three panels are in place, but in six months the structure will stretch across the bay. It will be massive and ugly, sure, but absolutely necessary according to government experts. Such walls are being built right up and down the Tōhoku coast, a vast project being proclaimed as the only way to tsunami-proof towns like Omori-wan for the future.

Hotaka understands what upsets Sakura so much. With all that money spent with so little to show, and so much more still to be spent on the seawall, she despairs of there ever being anything for proper housing, for ordinary people.

What can be done, though? Hotaka wonders. Matters like these have always been decided by the government and their advisors, big companies and so on. They're the experts, surely, not ordinary people. What do ordinary people know of such things?

Hotaka sighs. He really wishes he knew what to think.

He stares across the bay, the water a sombre dark blue. Ever since his grandfather started taking him sailing at a very young age, Hotaka has been keenly aware of the sea and its many moods.

'The sea is part of us,' the old man once said. 'We of the Tōhoku coast can never fully escape its grip.'

Hotaka feels the sea's sullenness, as thoughts of his grandfather gather round. How would Grandpa feel about what's happening to Omori-wan? What would he say? The old man had loved the little town and would've wept at the havoc harvested by the wave that took his life, along with many others.

Hotaka's grandfather had returned to Omori-wan that dreadful March day in 2011. He'd come on the worst possible bus, the one that arrived just before the earthquake hit. But he didn't run for the hills, it seems, as he'd always told Hotaka to do.

*You must have gone to the harbour, Jīchan, after the earthquake? Why? You knew there'd be a tsunami. You of all people knew. So why did you go there? What did you think you could do? Help people in your little sabani?*

Hotaka's grandfather loved that Okinawan boat. He'd built it with his own hands, under the watchful eye of a master boat builder. He kept it in perfect condition, and sailed it every chance he got, even at eighty years of age.

'It was his way of being at one with the sea,' Hotaka's mother told him through her tears when they found the old man where the tsunami had dumped him, twisted and broken, three kilometres inland, bits of his boat scattered nearby.

'If only you were here, Jīchan,' Hotaka whispers. 'You'd know how to rebuild the town.'

Uncle Yori would also know what to do, Hotaka thinks, and peers down at the harbour, picking out his uncle's trawler at once. The big blue and white boat is famous in Omori-wan, a symbol of survival, just as Uncle Yori is a kind of hero. He took on the wave and won. And they say he helped so many at sea in the turbulent, treacherous currents that accompanied the tsunami.

Hotaka makes a mental note to call on his uncle – they've not spoken in over a week – then turns and begins walking down the hill.

He's in no hurry, though. In fact he wouldn't care if he missed school completely. He began the day feeling upbeat, but that's faded now and he can feel himself sinking. Sakura's comments about Omori-wan haven't helped, but the Shaman Lady is mainly to blame. Her talk of the untethered one has really got under his skin. Hotaka doesn't want to go there; that's where sadness lives, unbearable sadness, the very last thing he wants.

If only he could snap his fingers and bring on tomorrow with its big soccer game. He doesn't want to be in today anymore. He decides to run, buoying himself with visions of victory on the morrow, scoring a goal at the very least. He sets off at a brisk pace, knowing that sadness is never far behind.

The rest of the day drags horribly for Hotaka. He does end up sinking to the low spot he'd hoped to avoid, and everything becomes hard work. Teachers get on his nerves, and he on theirs; the Maths teacher loses his temper and yells at him for not trying. Lessons are a bore, but time with his peers is even worse. Sakura tells him to take some happy pills. At least Osamu keeps his distance; they've both seen each other in their dark places, and know the need for personal space.

Even talking with Miss Abe doesn't help. She's delighted that the Shaman Lady will contribute to the Memorial Concert, and does a great impersonation of the old woman that makes Hotaka laugh. But it's not enough to keep the darkness at bay. She notices.

'What's wrong, Hotaka? You seem flat.'

That's one word to describe how he feels – the air has been sucked out of him. *Scared* is another word; *terrified* is best, terrified that if he's not careful every last breath of air will be stolen from him. It takes all his strength to stop himself from sinking further, into that truly suffocating blackness – a place of despair that many who've lived through the tsunami know only too well.

Everyone copes in different ways with what the tsunami did to them. Some are consumed by their ordeal, even to the point of ending their lives. Some rise above their grief. Some merely muddle on. Others learn to hide their pain behind a front, a mask; Osamu is one of those.

What of Sakura? How does she cope? Hotaka can't be certain because he knows so little about her, she's so secretive. Maybe that's it – secrecy. She keeps it all a secret.

And why not? After all, it's what he's done with Takeshi: kept him a secret. He thought it was such a well-kept secret, safe from prying eyes. But the Shaman Lady blew that one.

Far more difficult to deal with, though, is the Shaman Lady's insistence that he break his bond with Takeshi. She had no idea what she was asking. That would mean betrayal.

Takeshi is a lost soul. His body has never been found. He is still out there somewhere – his spirit in turmoil, wandering, untethered, unable to find peace. He needs an anchor. Without one his spirit would blow into oblivion. Hotaka is that anchor; if he broke the bond between them he would be abandoning his friend. He's already done that once, on the day of the tsunami; Hotaka still blames himself for allowing Takeshi to be stolen by the wave. He can't let it happen again.

After school, Hotaka avoids Osamu and Sakura, and rides home alone. He's pleased that his mother isn't back yet. She would pick up on his mood and pester him, when all he wants is to forget. He soaks in a long hot bath, then retires to his room with some food, leaving a note on the door:

### *Getting a good night's rest in prep for tomorrow's big match*

He buries himself in bed and hopes that sleep will visit him for at least some of the night.

# Thirteen

**Sleep does come, though not** the sort Hotaka wants. It's a sneaky sleep that plays cruel tricks, lulling him to slumber one moment, shaking him awake the next; clawing though his thoughts, preying on his mind.

He does eventually tumble into a deep sleep. But that proves even worse, for there he is ambushed by a nightmare. It's one he's had before, one from which he fears he might never wake.

*'Ready?' Takeshi whispers.*

*Hotaka swallows hard. He's staring into the sea thirty metres below, Takeshi at his side, their toes at the edge of the cliff.*

*'We agreed,' Takeshi insists. 'Today is the day. The big leap.'*

*'I know, but…'*

*'Forget the buts. Buts get in the way of everything.'*

*'It's okay for you. You're good at everything – and you've done this heaps.'*

*'Exactly, heaps. And am I injured? Not a scratch. It's all a leap of faith. Trust me.'*

*Hotaka wants to trust Takeshi. But it's a long way down, and the more he thinks about it, the more paralysed he feels.*

*'You've done it heaps too.' Takeshi points to a ledge halfway down the cliff. 'Only from a little lower, that's all. No big diff. Same leap, better buzz. And I mean mega better!'*

*Hotaka tries to steady his nerves. The sea is calm and inviting. He peers into its emerald depths and imagines sinking into its softness. But he cannot budge the wad of fear swelling inside.*

*'Come on. You can do it.'*

*Hotaka wants to believe his friend, but a voice says otherwise. He tries to take a deep breath, but his lungs won't let him. He tries to clear his head, but his mind won't be in it. He tries to make himself move, but his legs refuse. Buts! All those freakin' buts!*

*'Sorry, kid,' Takeshi says eventually. 'This dude can't wait any longer.' He steps backwards in slow, measured paces. 'The Great Ones are calling,' he yells, reeling off a list of sea gods and water spirits: 'Ryo-Wo! Watatsumi! Suijin! Isora! Mizuchi! I come to join you!'*

*Crouching low and clenching his fists, he springs forward.*

*'See you in heaven,' he shouts as he sprints past Hotaka, a huge grin across his face. 'Or hell!' he adds, thrusting himself from the cliff in a beautifully executed arc, plunging seaward like a spear.*

*Hotaka gasps, enthralled. Golden body glowing in the sunlight, slicing the air, piercing the sea with barely a splash, slipping seal-like into its deepest green. At one with the sea.*

*A moment later Takeshi surfaces, big wet face popping out of the water and beaming up.*

*'Come on, Hotaka,' he yells. 'Jump!'*

*Hotaka's legs are jelly, his stomach churns, and a wave of dizziness sweeps over him.*

*'Don't be a goose. Jump!'*

*But he cannot. He simply cannot. He closes his eyes, and that's when he hears Takeshi scream.*

*'Hotaka!'*

*When he opens his eyes again, the water below is no longer crystal clear but bruised black and blue, swirling with menace.*

*'Help me, Hotaka!'*

*Takeshi's face is ghostly pale, eyes iced with fear, lips of coldest blue. He reaches from the churning waters, his hand shaking.*

*Hotaka drops to the ground and hangs over the cliff as far as he can, reaching out to his friend.*

*'Take my hand,' he yells.*

*Despite the distance, their hands draw closer and closer, eventually touching. Hotaka feels Takeshi's hand in his, and grasps it tight. But there's no strength to his friend, no grip. Cold and wet, his fingers slowly slip away. Hotaka stares in horror as Takeshi's face is swallowed by the swirling menace, followed by his arm. His hand lingers for a moment on the surface before being sucked under.*

*'No!' Hotaka screams, stretching out. But there is nothing he can do.*

*And then he too is slipping, sliding into the blackness.*

'Hotaka!'

He wakes with a start, sweating, his head full of shouting. He sits up, sucking in a long deep breath, exhaling slowly. Calm. Be calm. A soft hand rests on his forehead for a moment.

'I'm okay, Okāsan,' he whispers into the grey light of dawn.

'You called out. A few times.'

'It was nothing.'

'You sounded—'

'It was nothing. Really.'

'It was him, wasn't it?'

Hotaka doesn't reply.

'That was so long ago, my son. You must let go.'

She's right, of course, like the Shaman Lady. 'I know, Okāsan, I know,' he replies. 'I will try.' He eases back onto his pillow, letting her stroke his brow.

'I saw the note on your door,' she says after a while. 'So it's a big match today?'

'Yeah. We need to win to stay in the comp. It won't be easy. The Samurai are top of the ladder.'

His mother's face darkens. 'Aren't they the ones that—'

'Yes, but I can handle them.'

'You didn't last time. They put you in hospital.'

'I was a year younger and a lot greener.'

'They'll do it again, Hotaka. I know they will.'

'They'll try. But I'll be ready. Football's a tough game. That's how it is, Okāsan.'

'Stop making excuses for them. It's got nothing to do with that. You know why they do it. They don't like you.'

'Come on. Who couldn't like me? I'm adorable.'

'You know what I mean. We haven't suffered enough.'

Of course Hotaka knows. In the first year after the tsunami people pulled together and helped each other. But since then progress has been slow and many have been left behind. Over the last year or so a growing envy has crept into communities all along the Tōhoku coast – envy of those who've got ahead, and of those who didn't lose their houses at all because they're rich and live higher up, above the tsunami line.

'Well, it's true. We haven't suffered like them. They lost everything.'

'You don't have to explain, Hotaka. Why do you think I do what I do? But envy is a cancer that festers into hate, and hate is poisonous. The only way we'll climb out of the misery and despair this tsunami has created is by doing it together. No community can survive in an atmosphere of envy and hate.'

'You're right, Okāsan. But soccer is just a game.'

'No. For some it's a chance to get even.'

'You're sounding like an awful snob.'

'I don't care, Hotaka. You're all I've got. Just be careful. Okay?'

He hears the worry in his mother's plea, and regrets calling her a snob. He knows she's anything but. No one works as hard to help the helpless as she does.

'Don't worry, Okāsan. I'll be careful.'

After his mother has gone, Hotaka climbs out of bed and goes to his window, pulling open the curtains. The morning sun is hiding behind a cloud.

'Watch over me, Takeshi,' he whispers. 'Make sure they don't smash me up too bad, huh? And maybe help with a goal or two?'

The sun slides from behind the cloud and warms his face.

# Fourteen

**Only two minutes of extra** time left, a hundred and twenty seconds, every one of them precious.

Against all odds the Rangers have proved a match for the Samurai, the score one all. Both goals were kicked in the first half, the Rangers' one by Hotaka's fellow striker. Since then the Samurai have controlled play and been ruthless. The Rangers have held them off, mainly with loads of good luck, but are worn out now. In the last ten minutes the Samurai have landed four shots on goal, two seriously close. With the end in sight, they've ramped up the charge, putting almost the entire team in attack. The Rangers are in real danger of crumbling.

Hotaka has had some rough treatment from the Samurai. It's what he expects as a striker, but it has been relentless – bumped and thumped on the sly, knees and elbows rammed into his back, kicks to his shins and ankles, a punch in the guts when the ref wasn't looking, and blows to the head. He's taken it all in his stride; to react would be both pointless and unsporting.

'Come on, Rangers!' he calls out to urge on his team. But he's also letting them know he's ready for any ball they can send his way. He can put on real speed if need be, aware that there are only two Samurai defenders between him and their goal. To score against the run of play would be awesome.

As if on cue, a strike on the Rangers' goal bounces off the top rail into the keeper's hands. He spins round and kicks the ball down the field. Hotaka takes it and sprints away.

*You can do it!*

He hears Takeshi's voice and feels him at his side, locking into total concentration as he heads down the field. The goal posts are beacons beckoning him. He has his line of attack mapped out ahead, aware of the defenders rushing at him, the rest of the Samurai rapidly gaining. Twenty metres out, he weaves sideways as though intending to send a long pass to the other striker. But with two defenders charging at him, he pivots on the spot and wrong-foots the goalie with a killer kick. The ball curves beautifully towards the top right-hand corner of the goal. A winner for sure, he tells himself.

*Do it!*

Hotaka doesn't see if he scores. The two defenders slam into him. He crashes to the ground, trampled by one, crushed under the other, the air knocked out of him. Gasping, he tries to scramble to his feet, but the pain is too great. He slumps, groans, and falls into a semiconscious swirl. Faces peer, hands reach down, voices call. He blacks out.

A whirlpool of debris spills into his mind. A viscous

black wave more solid than liquid churns him into a world that wallows between life and death. A town obliterated. A whole town swallowed and masticated, spat out, spewed up – bits and pieces, parts of buildings, floating rooftops, household items, buckled boats, trees, logs, cars, trucks.

And people – squirming in among it all like worms. *People*.

'I tried.'

Hotaka hears himself calling, but at the same time sees himself. He's somewhere within that world, and yet he's within this one as well, for the veil between the two has worn thin. Arms rise from the rubble, wriggle and writhe, then slip out of sight. Cries for help echo all around. Screams mingle with weeping and wailing, crunching and grinding, the hissing of gas tanks, the howling of sirens, the roar of explosions and flares.

A mother's tortured face looms at him, arms outstretched, hands grabbing air as her two daughters are ripped away by the wave. Her animal howl chases theirs as she plunges after them. An old man drifts by, eyes peering at Hotaka for a moment, then sinking, unblinking, into murkiness. A body bumps lazily into a car and sprawls across its bonnet as though resting for a bit before rejoining the spew. A dog whimpers. A tiny girl cringes on a floating roof, shivering with fear and cold. An old woman clings to the edge of the roof, struggling to pull herself up. A flurry of snow scatters ice-cold confetti as the tremors continue, reminders rumbling up from the deep.

Hotaka knows it's pointless to look away. All this and much more is inside him and won't be denied. He has no choice but to stare at the grim parade, and soon the yokai is there.

'I wanted you to stop,' Hotaka calls. 'But you kept going.'

The legless spectre in its pure white kimono floats above the water, drifting towards him. The head is bowed, its long hair matted with seaweed, its eyes downcast, while two multicoloured flames, the telltale hitodama, flicker above the figure, bathing it in eerie light.

'Please don't blame me. I couldn't help you.'

The yokai drifts closer, elbows held at the waist, forearms reaching out, pale hands hanging listlessly. Barely a metre away, it stops and lifts its head. Hotaka gasps. Even though he's seen the face many times, its deep and utter sadness always steals his breath away.

'You wouldn't stop.'

The figure lifts its head slightly, then raises its right arm and stretches towards Hotaka. Breathless, he watches the thin translucent hand float across to hover above his shoulder. As it descends, he closes his eyes.

*It's okay*, the hand seems to say as it rests on his shoulder and sinks gently into his very being. *It's all okay.*

The touch is so light as to be barely perceptible, and yet it sends a wave of overwhelming emotion through Hotaka.

'No!' he shouts and sits bolt upright. 'No it isn't!'

'You're okay.'

Hotaka opens his eyes and looks around, taking a while to realise where he is – on the football field, surrounded by faces. His team members are among them, and right next to him is the team's doctor, his hand on Hotaka's shoulder.

'Someone must be watching over you,' he says. 'That was a nasty collision, but I've checked you all over and you're fine to go home.'

The crowd cheers and Hotaka's team chants: 'We won, we won!' He laughs and slowly stands, wincing.

The doctor steadies him. 'You'll be sore for a while, but this will help,' he adds, handing Hotaka a tablet. 'And the coach will drive you home. Tell your mother I'll call later to check on you.'

Hotaka would love to stay and celebrate with his team, but decides he'd best follow the doctor's orders.

# Fifteen

**Hotaka sleeps very well,** not waking until late the next morning. Stiff and sore, he's glad it's Sunday; no school, no demands. He rolls over and almost goes back to sleep, but remembers an important task he has to perform.

He pulls on a yukata and slippers, leaves his room and walks along the rōka, the narrow hallway around the outside of the house, warmed by the late winter sun.

Hotaka's home is a traditional Japanese-style house. His father always threatened to modernise the place in Western style, but his mother resisted. She loves the timeless style of the rooms with their tatami floors and sliding fusuma doors of wood and paper set around a sheltered internal garden.

'Besides,' she once declared, 'the house is full of ancestral spirits. To modernise would disrupt them. The place would become unlivable, untethered spirits wandering everywhere.'

Hotaka was not convinced that his mother believed this. He reckoned her talk of lost spirits was only to annoy his father. Whatever the case, Hotaka's father never again raised the idea, settling on the Tokyo apartment for his dose of modernity.

Hotaka comes to a small room, removes his slippers, slides open the door and enters.

'Ojīsan, honourable grandfather.'

He speaks quietly as he crosses the tatami floor in socks to stand before the butsudan, the household shrine. The cabinet, about the size of a large wardrobe, has a sombre beauty. Made of black lacquered wood and gilt, it is inlaid with carvings of human and animal figures in gold and mother-of-pearl. On one panel a monk surveys a mountain scene. A crane flies across another. A lion stalks its prey on a third.

Hotaka bows low when he reaches the butsudan, then sinks to his knees onto a zabuton, a flat cushion. He flinches, unsure which part of his body hurts most, and gazes up at the shrine.

A statue of the Kannon Bodhisattva – Goddess of Mercy – gazes back from the highest part of the shrine. Lower down a photograph of his grandfather looks out at him. On each side of the cabinet stand several ihai, ancestral spirit tablets of shiny black wood with gold inscriptions. Hotaka's mother has already laid the usual offerings that morning – flowers, a small bowl of rice, some tea and fruit. Hotaka lights a candle on the platform in front of him, and then a stick of incense, placing it before his grandfather's spirit tablet.

'Forgive me for disturbing you, Jīchan. But I have very good news.' Hotaka grins. 'Remember the team I told you of, the guys that play dirty? I said we'd be slaughtered. In fact *we* did the slaughtering! Beat them two-one. And who do you think scored the winning goal? That's right, Jīchan.'

Hotaka stares at the photograph – struck as usual by the gentle eyes of the old man – and a mist of sadness wafts over him. It's almost three years since his grandfather was taken by the tsunami, yet barely a day passes when Hotaka does not think of him. He misses him terribly.

Hotaka's earliest memories are of perching on his grandfather's knee listening to stories; there were so many. Then came the sailing. From very early on Grandpa took him sailing in his beautiful sabani boat. They fished far out to sea, feeling the ocean heave beneath them. Closer to shore they collected nori from the seaweed frames, or simply skimmed across the bay on a happy breeze. The old man loved the sea and everything about it. Everything.

Perhaps he loved it too much, Hotaka thinks as he gazes at the photograph. He wipes a tear from his face, and makes himself smile for his grandfather.

'They say the cheers could be heard as far as Rikuz-entakata when I scored that goal. All I heard was a loud throbbing in my head as I passed out. Like I said, they play dirty. But I didn't let them get to me. I took your advice: play the game, not the man, be honourable always. And it paid off.'

Hotaka resists the urge to punch the air.

'I'm told it was a beautiful goal, Jīchan, catching the keeper right off guard. You would have loved it. I so wish you could have seen…'

A thought flashes through Hotaka's mind. Maybe his grandfather did see the goal. Maybe he was there, at the game, watching. They say that those we love never really leave our side, he thinks, that their shadows are always near. Takeshi was there.

'Sorry for blabbing on.' Hotaka presses down on his hands, flinching as he rises. 'I'll leave you in peace.' He takes the small hammer from the butsudan and strikes a bell. Then he extinguishes the candle, stands, bows, and slowly backs away.

As he walks back along the rōka he decides that he'll spend the remainder of the day resting and recovering. He'll sleep all he can.

# Sixteen

**Hotaka is up bright and early** the next morning. He dresses for school, glad that his aches and pains have eased, and heads off for breakfast.

As he walks along the rōka he feels the chill in the air and is pleased to see that the kotatsu is set up, the low dining table heated from underneath, with a light quilt tucked all around to keep in the warmth. Breakfast is laid out; a tray for him and one for his mother on opposite sides of the table.

Hotaka bows and bids his mother good morning. 'Okāsan, ohayō gozaimasu.'

'Don't wait for me,' she says. She is finishing an ikebana arrangement, meticulously setting the final flowers in place.

He leaves his slippers at the door, crosses to the table and slides his feet under the kotatsu. Relishing the warmth, he glances over his breakfast. It's the usual: steamed rice, miso soup and a range of side dishes – salted salmon, rolled omelette, dried seaweed and fermented soybeans.

He hates those natto beans – they smell foul and taste worse – but his mother never gives up pressing them on him. 'So good for you.'

Hotaka dips a few strips of seaweed into the soy sauce and folds in some rice.

'You're up early,' his mother says.

'Stuff to do,' Hotaka mumbles through his food. 'Before school.'

'Homework?'

He shakes his head. 'I have to see Mr and Mrs Suda.'

'The Puppet People?'

'Yes – they're the star attraction of our Memorial Concert.' He sips the miso soup and scoops up rice with his chopsticks.

'But they live up in the hills on the other side of the bay,' his mother says. 'That's thirty minutes away.'

'That's why the early rise,' he replies, downing the rice in a few mouthfuls.

His mother finishes the ikebana and joins him at the table. 'I could drive you,' she suggests, pouring him some green tea.

'No, thanks. Good training. Keeps me fit.' He drinks the tea, swallows some fried tofu and finishes the salted salmon. 'That was great, Okāsan. Just what I need for a long ride.' He pushes up from the table. 'Gotta fly.'

'Wait,' his mother says, pointing at the fermented soybeans. 'What about the natto?'

'I kept them for you. That's how thoughtful I am. What a good son, eh?' He grabs an apple, kisses his mother and leaves.

Hotaka hurtles down Monk Head Hill to the harbour-front. A little way along he turns into the street where Sakura lives with her aunt and uncle. He's never actually been inside the house because Sakura has never invited him; she can be cagey like that. But he's met her aunt and uncle, and he knows the house. It's a tiny prefabricated unit identical to many throughout the town – except for the flowers. Sakura's aunt loves flowers.

'They're sent to remind us of the good things in life,' she once told Hotaka.

In a plot of land at the front of the house Mrs Kita has planted every inch and has something flowering in each season. At present the Japanese apricot is in bloom and the plum blossoms will burst forth before long.

He slows down as he passes the house, wondering if Sakura is up yet. He'd love her to come with him to see the Puppet People, but decides not to call in; it would be intruding. He rides on, soon realising what a little oasis of colour he's left behind in Mrs Kita's garden. A handful of places have been painted, but most are either dull concrete grey or a mix of metal and rust. And none has flowers.

Halfway across town he comes to an area that still hasn't been cleared since the tsunami. Among the rubble squat dirt-smeared children, some throwing bits of masonry at a derelict house covered in graffiti. They give chase as Hotaka passes, hurling bits of debris at him.

He pedals faster and is soon climbing the escarpment road out of town. When he reaches the top he doesn't look back, but keeps riding until he reaches what he reckons must be the Puppet People's house. There is a large bunraku warrior puppet sitting on the roof clutching a welcome sign.

The house makes Hotaka smile, built as it is out of bits scavenged from the tsunami. The front is the bow of a fishing trawler, masts from wrecked boats providing uprights and crossbeams. A large Coca-Cola sign fills part of the front wall. Most of the windows are portholes. A freight container makes a workshop, and the whole house is finished off in a mix of colours as if there wasn't enough of any one paint to do the job. Hotaka's smile broadens and soon he's laughing at this masterpiece of mishmash.

He hops off his bike and leans it against the fence, with cries of *Go Oniwaka!* echoing in his head.

He hasn't seen the Puppet People since the day of the tsunami. They disappeared from public life for ages, hiding here, rebuilding their broken lives. Only in the last year or so have they resurfaced. When Miss Abe heard they were making puppets again, she had to have them in the concert. Hotaka can't wait to see them.

He walks through the gate and up to the front door, wondering what awaits him.

# Seventeen

**The beast stares at Hotaka** with the eyes of a killer. It is covered in scales, large armour plates over its chest and torso, sharp spiky ones down the back and along the tail, knobbly scales on its powerful arms and legs. The creature pulses and glows, as though smouldering with an eerie energy. Crouching low, it growls and opens its mouth, baring a tangle of jagged teeth. Then, in one rapid move that catches Hotaka by surprise, it springs forward and lashes at him with razor-like talons. He shrieks and stumbles backwards.

Then he bursts out laughing.

'Fantastic,' he shouts, clapping. 'The audience will love it.'

'Thank you, wakaino, young man,' two voices reply in unison from behind the creature.

The beast is in fact a large puppet of the bunraku kind, over a metre tall. It roars fiercely for a moment, thrashing its tail, then slumps, lifeless. Mr and Mrs Suda step forward, dressed entirely in black, balaclavas on their heads. Their darkened faces are just visible against the black backdrop – round, smiling faces. They bow together and step off the stage, handing the creature to Hotaka.

'It's *amazing*,' he says. 'And so real.'

'Yes, we're quite pleased with this one, aren't we, my dear?' Mr Suda nods to his wife and she nods back. 'Very Godzilla-like, but then he's meant to be. Think nuclear disaster, Fukushima and all the nightmares unleashed there by the tsunami. He's the main villain in our little tale.'

'Wonderful,' Hotaka says. 'It's perfect!'

'Naturally there's a princess,' Mrs Suda adds. She holds up a beautiful dark-eyed puppet wearing an elegant courtier's kimono. 'She represents Japan, ravaged by the nuclear beast.'

Mr Suda continues, 'The beast is abetted by a nasty mob of politicians, electricity executives and yakuza gangsters.' He opens a box of glove puppets and holds up a few. 'This one bears an uncanny resemblance to Mayor Nakano, don't you think?' The old couple giggle together. 'We'll need some students to help make these come to life. What a deliciously bad bunch. Poor Princess Japan.'

'But fear not, wakaino,' Mrs Suda shouts theatrically. 'The princess is rescued from evil by our hero. Ta *da*!' She presents a dashing samurai-like figure in black and red lacquered armour, with an ornate golden helmet.

'He represents the *people* of Japan,' Mr Suda explains. 'Ordinary folk rising up to fix the nation's woes.' He turns to Hotaka with raised eyebrows. 'Yes, I know: over-symbolic and very political. But such things need to be said. We've allowed ourselves to be bullied by politicians, businessmen and crooks for far too long in this country. I just hope it won't ruffle too many feathers at the school. We'd hate to cause you any trouble. Then again, if anyone should be radical in these troubled times, it's young folk like yourself. After all, you have the most to lose. So what do you say?'

'I love it,' Hotaka replies with a laugh. And he knows that Sakura will love it, too. Just the sort of stuff she's passionate about.

Mr and Mrs Suda beam with delight. 'We knew you'd understand,' they reply as one.

Hotaka beams, too; that's the effect these people have on him. In their company it's impossible not to feel that life is good. And yet they suffered as much as any in the tsunami. They lost everything that day, a lifetime of work and creation. The Wave took it all – workshop, theatre, musical instruments, sculptures, puppets, the lot – tore their home and business from the foundations and shredded it all. It nearly took their lives too, both swept away like over-sized puppets. She woke on the floor of a makeshift hospital. He was found down by the harbour, wandering in the dark, coated in mud. How they've managed to keep such high spirits is beyond him.

Hotaka hands the puppet back to Mr Suda. 'Everyone will love the play. I cannot thank you enough.'

'Be warned,' Mr Suda says, 'it will be our first public performance since the tsunami. We'll be rusty.'

'Be as rusty as you wish, Suda-san. What you call rust is gold dust to us.'

'Very good, wakaino. What a poetic compliment.'

Hotaka could stay all day with the old couple; they make him feel whole. But he suddenly sees the time and realises he'll have to ride fast to catch the second period. He must not be late. It's Maths! The subject's not the worry, the teacher is. Mr Tamura is old and cranky and, like Principal Hashimoto, lives by the rules. He demands that every student be at their desk when he walks into the room, books ready. Latecomers pay dearly unless they have a watertight excuse.

He apologises profusely to Mr and Mrs Suda, and leaps onto his bike.

# Eighteen

**By the time Hotaka gets** to school, the second period is about to start. He drops his bike and runs to his locker, yanks off his shoes, pulls on his school slippers, grabs his books and heads for class as fast as he can go. He sprints down the main corridor and slides around the corner, straight into the path of Mr Hashimoto, skidding to a stop centimetres from the principal and dropping his books.

'Whoa!' Mr Hashimoto holds up his hands. 'What's going on?'

'Gomen nasai, Principal Hashimoto! Please forgive me.' Hotaka scrambles about on the floor, collecting his books. 'I was rushing because I don't want to miss my favourite subject.'

'I see. And what might this *favourite* subject be?'

'Maths, sir.'

'Ah. With Tamura-san?'

'Yes, sir. He's such a great teacher. He always gives us such interesting problems. One of the great joys of, er, Maths.'

'Really? Tell me something, Hotaka. I have a strong feeling that you've only just arrived at school. Am I correct?'

Hotaka sighs. 'Yes, sir.' He fidgets and stares at the floor.

'An explanation, if you please.'

Hotaka could tell the simple truth, that he was doing stuff for the Memorial Concert. But according to school rules he should have *written* permission from one of the teachers. He doesn't have it – and Mr Hashimoto lives by the rules.

'I'm waiting.'

'Please don't be hard on the student, Principal Hashimoto.'

Hotaka is instantly relieved when Miss Abe appears.

'Allow me to take any blame. He was on a mission for me, a special school matter I didn't want to bother you with, knowing how precious your time is.'

'And may I ask what was this mission was, Abe-sensei?'

'Certainly, Principal. But perhaps Hotaka himself should deliver the good news.' Miss Abe gives Hotaka a *do-something!* stare.

'Of course, Abe-sensei,' Hotaka replies, turning to the principal. 'As you know, sir, I have been working with Abe-sensei and others to organise a special concert as part of the school's—'

'Yes, yes, I know all that. The good news – what is it?'

Hotaka is in two minds. He could simply tell the truth: that he was with the Puppet People and that they've agreed to be part of the Memorial Concert. But he wants to *really* impress Mr Hashimoto, and feels that might not be enough to do the job. From something Miss Abe once said, however, he thinks he knows what will be enough. So he decides to play with the truth a little.

'The reason I'm late this morning is that I visited Kosaki-san to make sure she'll sing at our concert.'

'The geisha?' Mr Hashimoto replies. 'I thought she said she'd never sing again?'

'Correct, sir,' Hotaka continues, a smile forming. 'But I have persuaded her otherwise. This morning she finally agreed to sing at our concert.'

Mr Hashimoto is delighted. To actually have a geisha at the Memorial Concert is marvellous enough for him. But to have one of such fame as Miss Kosaki is wonderful beyond words. He claps several times, and for a moment looks as if he might break into a little dance. But then he manages to contain his excitement.

'Is it really so?' he asks in a controlled whisper.

Hotaka nods, but inwardly gulps, knowing he'll just have to make it so.

Mr Hashimoto beams. 'When I was your age, I heard the great Kosaki-sama sing and I will never forget it.' He clears his throat before continuing. 'Her voice was a piece of paradise.' He pats Hotaka on the shoulder. 'Well done, wakaino. Well done.' He takes a deep breath and steps back, resuming a principal's decorum. 'Off you go, then.'

'There's just one small matter, sir. I am late for class now, and Tamura-sensei will not be pleased.'

'Quite right, Hotaka.' Mr Hashimoto strokes his chin. 'Tell him you've been talking to me.'

'Thank you, sir,' Hotaka says and heads off to class.

'I'll see you at lunchtime,' Miss Abe calls after him. 'You do know you're on lunch duty this week?'

'Sure do, Abe-sensei,' he replies, even though he had completely forgotten. *Great*, he groans internally, *a whole week of serving lunches to the other students.*

When Hotaka reaches the door to his classroom he knocks lightly and, after a pause, enters. He is greeted by a sea of faces. The only person not looking at him is Mr Tamura; he is writing up a problem on the board. He stops in the middle of an equation, his chalk pressed against the board.

'Did I tell you to enter, Yamato?' he says without turning around.

'I'm sorry, Tamura-sensei,' Hotaka replies. 'I thought I heard you—'

'Hearing voices now, are we? First sign of madness, you know.'

'Yes, sir. I mean, no, sir, I didn't know this, about madness, that is. But yes, sir.'

The class laughs. Hotaka's face feels extremely hot.

'And you're late. Nine minutes and forty-three seconds late, to be precise.'

'Yes, sir. I'm sorry but I—'

'What do you think that's a sign of?'

'Stupidity,' someone calls out.

Mr Tamura ignores this. 'Bad manners,' he says, scratching an equal sign on the board. 'Very bad manners.' He taps his chalk on the board for each word. 'Unless, of course, you have an excuse.'

'I do, sir. I was with the principal. He told me—'

'Enough,' Mr Tamura snorts, his piece of chalk snapping against the board. 'Sit down.'

Hotaka sighs. As he walks to his desk near the front of the class, he looks over at Sakura and Osamu, and gives them a thumbs-up. He doesn't see the foot shoot across his path. He is sent sprawling, his books airborne; one hits Mr Tamura in the back. The Maths teacher turns and glares at Hotaka on the floor.

'I said *sit* down. Not lie down.'

As Hotaka gathers his books, he glances back and quickly realises who tripped him. Tarou Nakamura – the class bully – is looking straight at him, a smug sneer smeared across his face. Hotaka returns the stare and holds it for a while before sitting.

# Nineteen

'**I always think I look stupid** in this gear,' Osamu says.

'You do,' Sakura replies. 'But then you look stupid in everything.'

'Very funny.'

Hotaka, Osamu and Sakura are all dressed the same: white coats, white face masks and white hats that look like shower caps. They're part of the same han group – an organised team of students whose job it is to keep the school clean and tidy, and to serve lunch.

They've just collected the lunch trolley with its fold-out serving table and are wheeling it back to their home classroom, where the other three members of their Han group will help serve lunch to the rest of the class and then clean up. That's their job for the week; they are on lunch-serving duty.

'I'll tell you who *did* look stupid this morning,' Sakura continues, nodding towards Hotaka.

He is deep in thought. About Tarou Nakamara, the guy who tripped him in Maths. The thug has been niggling Hotaka for months; mostly little stuff – dirty looks and snide asides – never any real challenge. Today's stunt was a definite ramping-up, and Hotaka is wondering how he should react. He's taller than Tarou, but no match in physique. He wouldn't like to get into a fight with him, but he won't be pushed around either.

Sakura raises her voice. 'I said, I'll tell you who *did* look stupid this morning.'

Osamu grins. 'Anyone I know?'

Hotaka pushes the trolley harder, and soon they reach their home classroom.

The next fifteen minutes are busy for Hotaka and his Han group as they serve the meals. Lunch is eaten in the classroom, so the students file by with trays, everyone receiving essentially the same lunch: fish with rice and vegetables, plus miso soup, a carton of milk and a piece of fruit.

Hotaka is at the end of the serving table, ladling out the soup. It's the same repetitive ritual: with each person he bows and takes their bowl, fills it with soup, and bows as he hands it back. They thank him politely. 'Arigatō gozaimasu.'

'You're welcome,' he replies. He takes the next bowl, and so it goes.

Being in his last year of junior high school, Hotaka has served many lunches, and is soon doing the job mindlessly, unaware of anything.

'That's not enough.'

A gruff voice snaps him from his daze. Tarou Nakamara is holding out his tray.

There is plenty in his bowl, but Hotaka reaches across with more soup. As he does so, Tarou tips his tray so that his whole lunch slides off onto the serving table and the floor.

'You idiot,' Tarou shouts. 'Why'd you do that?'

'What are you talking about?'

'You leaned on my tray.'

Almost immediately Miss Abe appears. 'What's the shouting about?'

'He made me drop my lunch,' Tarou says.

Miss Abe holds up both hands. 'I'm sure it was an accident.' She turns to Hotaka.

It was no accident, but Hotaka decides against making a scene. He is on lunch duty, after all. It's his job to serve.

'I'm sorry,' he says, looking Tarou in the eye. 'It was an accident. Please accept my apology.'

Tarou grunts begrudgingly, and Hotaka is about to leave it at that. But then he catches the snicker in Tarou's tone, and changes his mind.

'Allow me to get you another lunch,' Hotaka says. 'It's the least I can do.' He goes to the head of the queue, takes a tray and begins stacking it with food, double helpings of everything as he works his way down the line. By the time he reaches Tarou, the tray is piled ridiculously high. 'There now,' Hotaka says with just the hint of a sneer. 'That should be enough for a big boy like you.'

Tarou nods, but Hotaka can see that he's seething with anger. He knows Hotaka is making a fool of him. He takes the tray and backs away.

'Be careful,' Hotaka calls. 'We don't want any more lunches on the floor.'

'Whoa, man,' Osamu whispers. 'You just made one big enemy.'

'No. I just decided not to take crap from a dropkick.'

*One big enemy.*

Osamu's words echo in Hotaka's head during after-school sport. All through his ten minutes of kendo warm-up exercises, he definitely notices Tarou eyeing him off. As he prepares for the training and combat session, he sees Tarou talking to the instructor and nodding towards him. Hotaka is certain he's planning something.

*Of course.* It hits him. Tarou is getting himself paired with Hotaka for a combat session. A little friendly match, he's probably telling the coach. Yeah, real friendly, one in which Tarou will no doubt thrash him. He's capable of it. Hotaka is only a beginner; Tarou has been doing kendo for years.

Hotaka hopes it's not the case as he dons his body armour – the waist and side protectors, breastplate, helmet and grille with neck, throat and shoulder pads. The gear protects against strikes and thrusts from the shinai, the bamboo sword with which they fight, but hard hacks and jabs still really hurt. And Tarou is a vicious kendōka; Hotaka has seen him in action. He also fights dirty, attacking unprotected parts of the body whenever he gets a chance. It's against the rules, of course, and penalised in proper competition, but it's not hard to make such slips look unintended. And when it's just a friendly after-school knock-about, who's watching anyway? Hotaka knows he'll be slaughtered.

He pulls on his kote, long padded gloves, takes his bamboo sword, and joins the other kendōka in the middle of the gym for the group training session. There are sixty of them in neat rows and columns. Everyone looks much the same in their black jackets and trousers, faces hidden under grille helmets, with only slight variations in the colour of gloves, torso covers and breastplates.

Hotaka takes his position, then looks around for Tarou. His heart immediately sinks when he realises that that the guy is right behind him. He knows by the breastplate; it's a rich crimson, the only one of its kind in the group. Tarou is out to get him all right, and he's starting with a bit of intimidation.

*Ignore him*, Hotaka tells himself as the exercise session kicks off. He normally loves the kendo exercises, completely losing himself in all the noise and action. Everyone screams their kiai, battle cry, lashing out with bamboo swords, repeating a mix of short sharp strikes, long sweeping blows and lethal thrusts. They practise foot movements: the slow sliding steps as you size up your opponent, the rapid stamping steps of attack, and the sudden leap that catches the foe off guard. Over and over they repeat these actions together – sixty kendōka moving as one – chanting, yelling, striking, thrusting, sliding, stomping. It's a great release of energy and tension.

But not for Hotaka. Not today. Today the only thing he's aware of is Tarou, right behind him. He can feel the eyes burning into his back. He can hear the boy's kiai, louder than anyone else's, full of aggression. And he's aware of every strike and thrust of that shinai, some so close that Hotaka can feel the wind on the back of his neck.

*You just made one big enemy.*

Osamu's words echo in Hotaka's head, but he pushes them away.

*No. I just made a decision.*

That's it! He suddenly sees everything clearly. Tarou is not going away. In fact, the more Hotaka tries to ignore him, the more aggressive he'll become. The thug will have to be faced eventually. And a combat bout straight after this practice session is as good a time as any.

*No more crap from that dropkick.*

So instead of being worn down by Tarou's intimidation, Hotaka is fired up by it. He hears Tarou's blood-curdling kiai, and yells over the top of it with a howl that's longer and louder. He sucks in the air as Tarou's shinai whooshes behind him, and hacks down with his own weapon, slicing an imaginary foe in half.

*No more!*

By the time the practice session ends, Hotaka is as ready as he can be. He feels the tap on his shoulder, but before Tarou can formally challenge him, he spins round and gets in first.

'Onegai shimasu,' he says.

It's so very polite, this veiled invitation to fight.

# Twenty

'**You should've seen him, Sakura.** He was awesome.'

Hotaka doesn't feel awesome as he hobbles home with his two friends. His feet, his ankles and both upper arms are all bruised where Tarou struck hard with his shinai. One elbow is throbbing and his back and ribs are sore from some nasty jabs delivered on the sly.

'Tarou committed one foul after another,' Osamu says. 'He would've been disqualified ten times in a proper match. Hardly a legal hit the whole time.'

'He knew he could get away with it,' Hotaka explains. 'Coach was on the other side of the gym, his back to us all the time. We were only meant to be *practising* together. But Tarou went ape. It only took a few minutes, four at the most, but it had nothing to do with kendo. He was out to hurt me; and he did it while the coach's back was turned. All I could do was fend him off as best I could.'

'You did more than that, bud. You deflected heaps of his strikes but you also scored a few top hits. He wouldn't have expected that.'

'He didn't; I saw the surprise in his eyes when I scored that first whack on his helmet. He'd let his anger over-rule his mind, and he knew it. But that only made him wilder.'

'Sure did. He got really brutal near the end. I'm amazed you put up with it.'

Hotaka could have pulled out or protested. But he'd made up his mind at the start to see it through, whatever. It was all about personal honour. Do it properly, kendo style – 'the way of the sword'.

He could have played dirty, too. But he refused to, and that actually injured Tarou more than any blows Hotaka might have achieved by cheating.

When the session was over, Hotaka was very relieved indeed. He couldn't have hung on much longer, and he left the floor incredibly sore. But he also felt he was the real winner.

'You're a hero in my eyes,' Osamu says as he hops on his bike. 'See you later,' he shouts, and pedals off.

Hotaka and Sakura walk on in silence. He senses a coolness in her, and wonders about it. Only when they're almost at the harbourfront does he eventually speak.

'You're quiet, Sakura. You haven't said a thing since we left school.'

'Haven't had a chance. Osamu's been singing your praises nonstop. He worships you. How come? Did you save his life or something?'

Hotaka laughs. 'Don't be silly.' He blushes. 'But yeah, he does go on a bit. I wish he wouldn't.'

'Liar. You love it. You'd be feeling very pleased with yourself right now.'

'I don't know what you mean.'

'Come on, admit it. Wounded warrior, honourable to the end in true kendo spirit. Hotaka good guy, Tarou bad dude. Am I right?'

Hotaka bristles. 'Well, I didn't cheat, if that's what you mean.'

'Of course you didn't. Honourable Hotaka cheat? Unthinkable! You couldn't cheat to save your life.'

'Hang on, am I supposed to feel bad about *not* cheating?'

'No. But nor should you think yourself better. You don't know how to cheat because you've never *had* to. That's the difference between you and Tarou.'

'What's with the lecture?' Hotaka asks. 'What are you getting at?'

'It's simple.' Sakura points ahead, to the hill where Hotaka lives. 'The tsunami didn't touch you; you've still got your house and all the stuff that makes up your memories and who you are. Tarou has nothing, not even a photograph. Father swept away, never found. Mother an alcoholic mess. Where you live the air is fresh. Tarou lives with the dust and fumes, stuck in a shipping container. You're cosy all year; he swelters in summer, freezes in winter. Sure you suffered some personal loss in the tsunami, like Tarou. The difference is that you were in a position to get on with life once the disaster was over. Not Tarou – he hasn't even begun recovering. Three years have gone and he still doesn't know where to start.'

Hotaka is about to reply, but Sakura continues.

'See, I know Tarou. He lives only two streets away. We've spoken a few times. He never says much, but I've picked up enough to know that he's not bad, just confused. When he whacks you with his shinai he's hitting out at something that scares him. He sees a big gap between people like you who have pretty much everything, and people like him with nothing. He sees that gap widening every day and it freaks him out.'

Sakura steps right up to Hotaka.

'So when you came away from kendo feeling good about yourself for standing up in an honourable fight against a cheat, you were wrong. In fact you were actually fighting a frightened mixed-up kid who's having trouble just getting life to make sense.'

'Okay, okay!' Hotaka throws up his hands. 'I get it. I surrender. You've trashed my ego, but I get it. What I don't get is why you're so obsessed with this. It's like you're on a crusade. What's your point?'

They reach the T-intersection on the harbourfront where they would normally part company, but Sakura grabs Hotaka and shakes him.

'Do you really want to know?' she shouts. 'Do you?'

'Yeah,' Hotaka shouts back. 'You bet I do.'

'I'll show you then.' She grasps his hand and drags him across the road.

# Twenty-one

**Hotaka can feel the tension** in Sakura as they cross to the harbourfront.

'You're right I'm on a crusade. And you should be too. We all should be – me, you, Osamu, Tarou, everyone young and old in the Tōhoku region, but especially us – our generation.'

'Why?'

'*Because!*' Sakura shouts, as if that word alone is enough. Her eyes dart about – along the marina, out into the bay, to the town, the hills, the sky. 'Oh my god, there are so many becauses. Tarou and the many thousands suffering like him are part of it. But the problem is much bigger and deeper, Hotaka, particularly because it's not even seen as a problem by those in power.'

'Sorry, but I have no idea what you're talking about.'

'Let me spell it out, then. If we're not careful the whole Tōhoku area will be the centre of a man-made disaster that will make the 3/11 tsunami look like a picnic. And it's all happening under the guise of reconstruction. Our so-called big recovery is in fact a big con trick.'

'Oh, come on.' Hotaka points to the scene of reconstruction ahead. 'It looks ugly now, but it's rebuilding what was destroyed. Isn't that what recovery is about?'

'Of course we need the roads, the bridges, the streets, and all that stuff. But so much of it is happening in the wrong places. Down here is the past.' Sakura points to the slopes rising from the coastal flats. 'Up there is where we should be rebuilding. Down here should be for agriculture, for storage and warehouses, maybe even industry. Not somewhere for people to live, not in large numbers anyway.'

'But this is where the town has always been, for centuries.'

'Exactly. And how many times has it been washed away? Three that I can think of in the last one hundred and fifty years. We've got recorded tsunamis in this area going right back to 869! They're part of our history. You'd think we'd have learned our lesson by now.'

'That's why we're building the seawall.'

'Aahhh!' Sakura glares across to where construction of the wall has begun. 'That is the worst bit of all. Those three concrete panels might look harmless now, but that wall will stretch right across the bay, cutting off any view of the sea. What's the point of living by the ocean if you build a wall that stops you seeing it? And this is happening all along the Tōhoku coast. Hundreds of kilometres of ugly concrete walls costing billions of yen. For what?'

'To stop the next tsunami, of course.'

'Hello! We wouldn't need any walls if towns were built higher up. But in any case the seawalls are crap. Most of them were useless against the 3/11 tsunami. Even the biggest walls failed, and some made the effects of the tsunami worse. I'm talking facts here. Only one of all those walls actually saved the community behind it. The wave just went over the top of the others, or smashed through them. And one of the reasons so many people died is that they thought the walls were fail-proof. They weren't.'

'Yeah, well that's why they're building the walls bigger this time, and stronger and higher.'

'It will never be enough, Hotaka. *Never!* Nature will always make fools of us if we try to beat her that way. We have to be smarter, not bigger and tougher. We have to learn from our mistakes, not repeat them. What we're doing here is plain stupid.'

'But the experts and the government all say—'

'Experts? Government? You don't honestly believe them, do you? They're liars. Look at what's happening around Fukushima – endless lies as poisonous as the radiation leaks. And it's no different here. The crazy part is that we keep believing them, we the ordinary people of this country.'

'Hey, Sakura! It's not that bad.'

'It is! In fact it's worse. The Tōhoku region is living a huge lie. The seawalls aren't for the people. They're for big business, and for all the politicians in league with big business.'

Hotaka has never seen Sakura so fired up. She's been angry plenty of times before, but this is different. Her voice is pitched with urgency, the words pouring out, her finger jabbing the air. He stares at her in amazement. People in the street stop and stare too. When Hotaka sees this he can't help smiling.

She's just like a politician herself, he decides, the very sort of person she's ranting and raving about. He holds back a chuckle, but it's no good; the picture has lodged itself in his brain and won't go away. He can just see her in the national parliament, the Diet, shouting her views, shaking her fist and laying down the law. And before he can stop himself, he's laughing.

Sakura glares. 'What's so funny?'

'You.'

'What do you mean?'

'Sorry,' Hotaka splutters. 'I can't help it, honest. You see, I've got this mental picture of you, and, and...' He doubles up with mirth.

'Stop,' Sakura shouts, her face bright red. 'Stop it!'

Hotaka manages to keep a straight face for a few seconds. But one glance at Sakura sets him off again, gripped by fits of laughter.

Sakura's face drops, the colour draining from it, and Hotaka knows he's gone too far.

'How dare you,' she whispers, her lips quivering, eyes glistening.

'I didn't mean—'

'How dare you treat me like a fool, a child throwing a tantrum.'

'It's not like that. I wasn't—'

'I expected more of you. I'm pointing out a terrible

crime here that's being committed against our generation – all these old politicians spending mountains of money that we will have to work like slaves to pay back. I thought you would at least listen, maybe even try to understand. Isn't that what friends do for each other?'

'I *am* your friend, and I—'

'No.' Sakura fights back tears, her voice faint and distant. 'You're so blind you can't even see what's in front of you. These people are stealing our future – yours, mine, Tarou's, Osamu's – and all you can do is laugh. That's terribly sad.'

She turns and walks away.

'Sakura! Wait!' Hotaka calls, but there's no point. All he can do is watch her go.

# Twenty-two

**Hotaka stares at the ceiling.** It's after midnight and he can't get to sleep. He's still hurting all over from Tarou's beating during kendo, but that isn't what's keeping him awake. Sakura is. He's hardly stopped thinking about her since they parted that afternoon.

'Kuso.' He curses under his breath.

Hotaka is struggling with two realisations. The first is how very much he cares for Sakura – not in a romantic way, although there might be some of that as well. But whatever else he might feel, his care for Sakura is *as a friend* first and foremost, a very important friend. He realised this the moment he saw how deeply he'd hurt her. His laughter crushed her in a few seconds. A simple laugh turned ugly and hurtful, shredding her trust, shattering their friendship.

'Kuso!'

Hotaka's other realisation is how very little he actually knows about Sakura. He and Osamu are definitely her closest friends, yet neither could say they really *know* her.

They've never asked about her past because she never invited them to; in fact she's actually thrown up a wall around herself. So they accept her as she is; no questions, even though Hotaka has often wished he knew more.

He still doesn't even know where she came from, almost a year later. No one does. 'South,' she once said dismissively when pressed. Asked how far south, her eyes clouded over. 'Nowhereville, okay?' she snapped and walked away. Osamu is convinced she's from Fukushima, a radioactive refugee. But that's only a guess.

And what of her parents? She's never spoken of them, not once. It was months before Hotaka discovered she was actually living with her aunt and uncle. He once glimpsed a photo that fell from her bag, of two adults, and guessed they must be her parents. He wanted to ask, but she instantly scooped it up.

Hotaka reaches for his phone again. He's done it several times, intending to call or at least message Sakura, only to back out at the last moment. He stares at the phone for a while, then shakes his head and tosses it aside. If only time could be turned back, he wishes, and rolls onto his side.

Hotaka rises early the next morning. He still feels a dull pain as he eats breakfast, but most of his aches have gone. He's also managed to push his worries about Sakura to the back of his mind; he's not sure how long that will last.

'Another busy day?' his mother asks.

He nods. 'There are still some performers I need to contact. The main one is the old geisha, Kosaki-san. I'm seeing her this morning before school. I also need to make sure the musicians are ready to go. And Abe-sensei has a collection of poems about the tsunami written by locals. Students will recite them between acts. I've got to email people about those, too.'

'Uncle Yori called, you know?'

'Really? I've been meaning to drop in, but never seem to find time. What did he want?'

'He wouldn't tell me. But he said it would be worth your while.'

'Worth my while? That sounds interesting. Wonder what it is?'

'There's only one way to find out, my son.'

The geisha is waiting for Hotaka. She waves from her window and greets him at the door.

'Welcome, wakaino, young man,' she says, with a warm and gentle smile.

He cannot believe she's eighty. Her skin is soft and smooth and her eyes glisten with a mischief mirrored in a cheeky smile. Hotaka feels immediately at ease.

'If my singing could return everything to what it once was,' she tells him, 'I would sing until my voice was no more. But we old geishas are a rare breed. Soon there will be nothing left of our old ways.'

'I can't agree, Kosaki-san,' Hotaka says with a smile. 'I bet that once you perform at our ceremony, there will be many young ones at your door.'

'Ha, wakaino!' She wags a finger. 'Flattery will get you everywhere.' She crosses to the window. 'Let me show you something.'

They gaze at a dismal scene of urban construction, across fields of dirt, weeds and tufty grass. A new road is being built, mostly still gravel. Trucks trundle by, throwing up dust and fumes. There are quite a few buildings, but most are temporary, prefab drab, utilitarian ugly.

'Out there is as far as the tsunami came. It was as if the gods drew a line through our town, right past my door. On that side, obliteration, death and destruction. On this side, everything left alone.'

She sighs.

'I used to boast about the view from this window: one of the prettiest parts of town. Over there was the best noodle bar in all of Tōhoku; next to it, Sato-san's shoe repair shop. A shameless flirt he was,' she adds with a giggle. 'Then a bookshop, a bakery, and Nakamura-san's confectionary shop; her wagashi were to die for.' She rolls her lips, reliving the little sweets. 'Further on, the tatami mat maker; a real pain in the bum, but I miss him. He was part of my life. I miss them all.'

Miss Kosaki pauses briefly, then hurries on, as if talking might keep the sadness at bay.

'My favourite flower shop was next; Toko-san's ikebana arrangements were made in heaven. And then...' The geisha's face drops. Her voice falters. 'And then the wave came.'

Hotaka takes the old woman's hand, so tiny, so delicate, and gently presses it. She regains some composure.

'All that was rubbed out.' She swipes her hand across the windowpane. 'Gone in minutes, turned to rubble and death. All the noises, the bustle and babble, the colours, the lights and lanterns, the flowers, gone. I can't tell you how many cherry blossom trees lined that street. Magnificent in spring. Gone. Ripped up at the roots. Erased.'

She turns away from the window.

'My voice was erased as well. Each morning I'd rush to the window, hoping the tsunami had been a bad dream. But each morning I'd gasp, and another piece of song would die in me. Eventually I fell silent, unable to sing in such a desolate place.'

'But you are singing again, aren't you?' Hotaka asks hopefully. 'Abe-sensei said you were, and that you'd sing at our school concert. Please says it's so.'

'Yes, I have my voice back,' the geisha replies. 'Thanks to a bird.'

'A bird?'

'Exactly. One morning I was woken by a tapping at my window, the sun barely up. On the ledge was a bush warbler, an uguisu. Drab little birds, but they bring in the spring, you know? This one had such a smiley beak that I opened the window. The tiny chap flew in and perched next to the heater. He eyed me up and down, puffed out his chest and sang for a full minute.

'His song was like a candle in the blackest of nights, and it made me realise something. Sadness is not necessarily the enemy of happiness. The two can live together. In fact sometimes they *need* each other – for the dark gives the light a place to shine. Anyway, when the little fellow finished I knew that I could sing again. In fact I knew I *had* to sing again. It was my duty to others.'

She smiles.

'I've kept you long enough. All I've really been saying in my roundabout way is that I can't wait to sing at your Memorial Concert.'

'Kosaki-san, arigatō gozaimasu. The honour will be all ours.'

As Hotaka rides off, he glances up at the little house where the old geisha lives. She's at the window again, waving. He waves back and as he continues on his way he hears her singing a popular old song, one that is sung every year around Children's Day in May.

In Hotaka's head her voice rises above the trucks and diggers and dozers until it is all he hears.

# Twenty-three

'**That leaves the poets** and the musicians.'

Hotaka is with Miss Abe, giving a progress report on final preparations for the school's Memorial Concert.

'Excellent, Hotaka,' she says. 'I'm especially pleased that the geisha will perform. I've already cleared things with the musicians, by the way. So it's only the poets to go.' She produces a folder. 'Here's all the information you need for them – poems, names, email addresses and so on. Do it in your spare time.' She laughs. 'Not that you'd have much of that. I fear I've seriously overworked you.'

'Not at all. It is a privilege to be part of this. As it happens, I have a free period now, so I'll get onto this at once.' He takes the folder, stands and bows.

'Oh, Hotaka,' Miss Abe calls as he walks away. 'Any idea where Sakura might be? It's not like her to miss a day at school.'

Hotaka shrugs. 'Sorry, Abe-sensei. No idea at all.'

He's wondered the same thing himself, but has been

trying not to think about it. He goes to a secluded part of the library and sits down with the poems. His job for Miss Abe is simple. All he has to do is lump the addresses together into a group email and send it off with the permission message she wrote for him.

But he makes the mistake of flipping through the folder, reading some of the poems.

*Barely ten years old,*
*The little boy*
*Pushes through the crowd,*
*Calling for his parents*
*Calling out their names for everyone to hear*

*Osamu!* He shudders, knowing he should stop, but he can't. Already captured. Like little traps, these poems. One more, he tells himself, and then the email.

But one more is too many. He knows it the moment he starts reading.

*Though terrified*
*That his name will loom*
*among the lonely lists of the dead,*
*I force myself to scour them*
*Each and every day*

Hotaka gasps. He tries to look away, to close his eyes, but can't. Tries to pretend he didn't read the words, but he did. Like a prisoner surveying his sentence, he reads the poem again, slowly, painfully. And as he does so, he can feel Takeshi behind him, leaning over his shoulder, pressing closer.

'I searched every day,' Hotaka whispers. 'All day, every day, I searched for you, right through the town, what was left of it, always sure that I'd find you wandering in a daze somewhere. But I didn't. And then I started searching the newspaper lists, the names. You weren't there either.'

Hotaka leans back in the chair, and feels the arms gently fold around him.

'There still isn't a day when I don't think of you, wonder where you might be. But then I'm sure you know that.'

He closes his eyes, trying to hold back the tears.

'Where are you, Takeshi? You must let us know so that we can put you to rest, set your spirit free. And so that our hearts can begin to mend, too. Please let me know, my friend. Please.'

The arms tighten around Hotaka with a softness that feels safe and secure, a cocoon of assurance that all will be okay. For the first time ever since the tsunami, he detects a sense of release from the past. It's only a shimmer, but it's a whisper of hope that leaves him feeling comforted.

'Thank you,' he sighs, and returns the poem to its folder.

'People often miss school,' Osamu says. He and Hotaka are pushing the lunch trolley along the corridor. 'Maybe she slept in. Maybe she wasn't feeling well. Girls have days like that, you know? It's—'

'I know, you dork. It's not that.'

'Maybe she's just being smart. Doesn't want to do lunch duty, so she stays home. I bet you that's it.'

'No. Sakura wouldn't do that. Anyway, there's still the text I sent her. She hasn't replied.'

'That doesn't surprise me. If you upset her as much as you told me, then she's hardly going to reply in a hurry.'

'I said I was really sorry.'

'Maybe you need to *show* her you're really sorry.'

For the rest of the day, Hotaka worries about Sakura. In the end he decides that Osamu is right. So as soon as school is out, he rides straight to Sakura's house.

He knocks at the front door, glancing about as he waits. His eye is caught by a small blue and red cement kappa, the mythical lizard-like creature said to inhabit ponds and rivers in the Tōhoku region. It stares up at him as though challenging his presence. He waits a moment longer, then knocks again. He knows that Sakura's uncle has a part-time job in construction, but is fairly sure her aunt doesn't work because of arthritis. Eventually he hears movement and soon the door opens a little.

'Good afternoon, Kita-san.' He bows.

'Hotaka,' Sakura's aunt replies, opening the door a little more. She stands as if lost for words.

'Please forgive me for intruding like this,' Hotaka continues. 'But I'm worried about Sakura. She wasn't at school today. Is she all right?'

'Yes! I mean, no. I mean she's all right now, but she wasn't. Before, that is. She was quite ill last night and, er, this morning.'

'I'm sorry to hear that. But she's okay now?'

'Um, yes. And no.' Mrs Kita gives a quick sideways glance. 'She's as well as can be expected.' Hotaka is about to ask if he can see Sakura, but her aunt continues. 'I'd invite you in but Sakura is asleep. I'd hate to disturb her.'

Hotaka smiles politely. He suspects that Sakura's aunt is not being totally truthful, from the edginess in her voice and the way she's holding the door so tightly. He decides that Sakura is on the other side of the door, and raises his voice accordingly.

'I understand, Kita-san. Please tell Sakura that I am very sorry indeed, and hope that she will be better for school tomorrow. If she likes, I will call in the morning and we can go together. Please tell her that.' He bows.

'Of course, Hotaka,' Mrs Kita replies. 'You are most kind.' She bows and closes the door.

# Twenty-four

**Hotaka heads down to the bay**, deep in thought. A truck blares its horn when he crosses the road to the harbour without looking. He gazes out over the marina, not really seeing anything, his mind still back at the little house. He's certain that Sakura was there, behind the door. But why would she hide? Surely she wasn't still angry with him?

He looks up. The afternoon sun is surprisingly warm for this time of year. A light breeze ripples the water, gently rocking the boats. Why can't everything be this simple, he wonders.

He's about to turn for home when he notices a group of people pointing at something and follows their gaze. They're pointing at the seawall. And no wonder; the three massive concrete panels are covered in graffiti.

The middle panel is crammed with all sorts of slogans in big red letters: ***Stop the Wall. Don't Imprison Us! Act Up! Seawall Bad Call. Let Us See the Sea. Don't Keep Nature Out.***

The panels on either side have only one slogan each, written in huge letters. **TEAR DOWN THIS WALL**, the first one shouts. The third panel exhorts: **STOP! BEFORE IT'S TOO LATE**.

It's her. Hotaka knows it at once. He can't imagine *how* she managed it – those panels are enormous. She must have had help. But that aside, there's no doubt in his mind; the graffiti are Sakura's work.

He laughs, unable to stop himself. Part of him wants to rush straight back to her house, bang on the door and congratulate her. But maybe her aunt was telling the truth; maybe she really was asleep. She'd have to be exhausted after doing all that. It would've taken ages, all night even. He stares incredulously at the huge concrete blocks, and pulls out his phone.

*OMG!* He begins a message to Sakura, but then hears his name.

'Hotaka.'

He recognises the voice and glances up from his phone. Uncle Yori is waving from his boat-shed. Hotaka waves back, and quickly finishes the message.

*Amazing! But how did you do it?*

He presses SEND, then crosses the marina.

'You've come at last,' Uncle Yori booms in his gruff fisherman's voice, a grin etched on his sun-tanned face. 'And about time. Hurry up, then! We'll manage a test run if we don't dawdle.'

'What do you mean?'

'Just hurry, boy! Time is of the essence.'

Uncle Yori heads into his boat-shed, Hotaka right behind him. It's dark, and his eyes take a while to adjust.

He almost bumps into his uncle when the big man suddenly stops and points.

'Well? What do you think of it?'

Hotaka squints. 'What do I think of—' He gasps, suddenly realising what he's looking at. 'No!' he shouts. 'I don't believe it.' He throws his arms around the fisherman. 'It's Jīchan's boat!'

'Not bad, eh? Even if I say so myself.'

'It looks perfect. How did you manage this? When did you—'

'Enough.' Uncle Yori waves his hands about. 'We can talk on the water. Come along, lad. Hop to it. Let's launch this craft.'

The little boat sails superbly, making the most of the light breeze.

'She's a real sabani,' Hotaka cries as they skim across the bay.

They've been sailing for over half an hour. The sun hangs above the hills to the west, its warmth fading fast now. Uncle Yori is on the main sail, Hotaka at the rudder, and he's really starting to feel as if he's getting the measure of the nippy little craft.

'I'd love to take her out there.' He nods towards the open sea.

'Me, too,' Uncle Yori replies. 'She'd handle it easily, no question. But not now, I'm afraid. In fact we'd best head back. That breeze is dying. I'd hate to be becalmed. It's a long row home.'

They go about and begin tacking towards the harbour.

'See how close she sails to the wind,' Hotaka remarks. 'Just like Jīchan's boat used to. How did you get it so right?'

'Well, I had photographs, and then I had help from the master boat builder who worked on the original boat. Time was the main thing. It took the best part of two years; whenever I got a spare moment I worked on it.' Uncle Yori slaps the boat affectionately on the side. 'But it's been worth it all just to see your face.'

'What you have done is so very special, Uncle. I can't tell you how special.'

Uncle Yori shakes his head. 'Good to hear. You see, I had to build this boat; I felt something was missing in my life without it. I did it in memory of the old man, as well, so that he would always be with us. And you know I think that he is with us now.'

Hotaka nods. He can feel his grandfather all around them – in the billowing sail, in the mast, the rudder, in all the loving care and attention to detail that's gone into the little boat. He can almost hear the old man's voice in the breeze: *It's in our blood, the sea. In our blood.*

'But more than anything I built it for you. Your jīchan gave you a love of the sea, we both know that. I know a large part of that love withered when the sea stole him. But I believe he would weep forever if you were to turn your back on the sea because of his death. I thought you'd never sail again unless I somehow lured you back. I decided this was the only way.' Uncle Yori grins. 'And it looks like I was right.'

Hotaka grins too. 'Totally.' A strong gust has come up; the sabani grabs it and sails beautifully. 'Totally right!'

The gust holds, taking them across the bay at good speed. They hang on, enjoying every moment. Only once they're close to the marina does the wind back off.

'Good timing,' Hotaka says as they glide sedately towards the marina. 'I think we've had the best of the wind for the day. We must do it again.'

'I'd love to. But more than anything, *you* must do it again. Alone, or with a friend, I don't care. Consider the boat yours, to sail whenever you wish.'

'But that's impossible. You can't—'

'Don't argue, lad. It's what your jīchan would've wanted. That's why I built the boat. And that's why you must accept it as yours.'

Hotaka has a lump in his throat. 'I don't know what to say.'

'Then don't say anything.'

They pull into the marina and slide alongside Uncle Yori's boat-shed. Hotaka douses the sail and looks about. The sun is sinking and there's already a chill in the air, but Hotaka has never felt so warm inside.

'Beautiful, eh?' Uncle Yori says, laying his hand on Hotaka's shoulder. 'And yet the sea can be so violent. That's Nature for you. One moment it cradles us like babies; the next moment it crushes us.'

They stand for a while, taking in a wide sweep of the bay, their eyes eventually resting on the seawall.

'That's why whoever did the graffiti knows exactly what they're talking about. We're part of Nature. We can't shut it out with walls. We have to live *with* it, not against it.'

'Hang on. Are you saying we don't need the seawall?'

'You bet I am. It's a hugely expensive joke...on *us*, the people of Omori-wan. The ones laughing are those pocketing the money – construction companies, corrupt politicians, the yakuza, but especially Mayor Nakano and his sidekicks. The whole reconstruction program is out of control, but that wall is the worst part. It should not be happening.'

'So why haven't you ever said anything? Why hasn't *anyone* said anything?'

'Good question. There are many reasons, but no excuse. Heaps of people like me have been too busy rebuilding our lives since the tsunami to worry about anything else. Then the government put strict conditions on reconstruction funds, insisting we agree to the seawall before receiving any other money for the town. There's a fear factor, too – protesters are always silenced when big money is involved, and this is *huge* money. And then of course there's that weird attitude we Japanese have of always bowing to authority, always doing as we're told, never questioning. No wonder we get trampled by the big guys.'

'So what good is the graffiti, then? If we always do what we're told, what difference will it make?'

'A lot, this time. That graffiti will get people thinking. It's the fuse that could blow Mayor Nakano's corrupt little game sky high.'

Hotaka stares at the graffiti. It's Sakura's work, he's certain. That sends a shiver of pride and excitement right through him. His friend. So strong. So right.

'Of course, whoever did this is also very brave,' Uncle Yori continues. 'The mayor will do anything to quell it as quickly as possible.'

'You think so?'

'I know so. There's too much at stake here to let a bit of graffiti get in the way. He'll do *anything.*'

Uncle Yori's words send another shiver through Hotaka.

'That's why we can no longer stay silent. This is a chance to take back control of our own town. We cannot afford to lose that chance. We need to keep this fuse burning.'

'How?'

'Another good question. Sleep on it.' Uncle Yori slaps his nephew on the back. 'Let's see what tomorrow brings, eh? Every tree was once a tiny seed.'

Hotaka leaves his uncle and walks home pushing his bike, dizzy with elation. A little way up Monk Head Hill he stops and sends another message to Sakura.

*I am so proud of you. I hope you'll still call me your friend. See you tomorrow morning?*

## Twenty-five

**'You've really started something.'**

Hotaka is walking to school with Sakura. To his relief he received a text message overnight, saying she'd wait for him outside her house in the morning.

'There was a crowd at the marina when I came past, easily double that of yesterday. People were taking snaps of your graffiti, even selfies. My uncle says you've lit a fuse. He's right.'

'Sshhh.' Sakura nods over her shoulder at some students behind them.

Hotaka lowers his voice. 'It's really got people talking. And *thinking*, which is what you wanted.'

'Yes, but they need to act as well, and I'm not sure how to make that next *big* step happen.'

'If the reaction so far is any indication, Omori-wan could really run with this.'

'I hope so.' Sakura sighs. 'And yet I'm frightened that I've started something that will get too big for me. Whatever happens, I want you to realise that I had to do this. I had no choice.'

'I know. But you didn't do it alone, surely.'

'No way. It was a big job. Took most of the night.'

'I figured as much. So who helped?'

Sakura grins. 'Guess.' When Hotaka shrugs, she mimes a kendo move.

'*What?*' He looks around, then mouths the name: 'Tarou?'

Sakura nods.

'How come?'

'After I left you the other day, I was so fired up. I knew I had to do something, but couldn't work out what. I walked around racking my brain until it was dark. I gave up and was on my way home when I came upon Tarou and a few of his friends spraying graffiti down some back street. It hit me in a flash. The concrete panels were perfect canvas, Tarou the perfect artist.'

'Amazing.'

'Exactly. Tarou jumped at the idea, and late that night we did it. He got so fired up too, like he'd found a mission.'

Hotaka can't help noticing how tired Sakura looks. There are shadows under her eyes, and her face is pale. He realises how much she must have put into this thing, and how important it is to her.

'You got me thinking, too.' He reaches out with his eyes. 'You were right the other day and I was wrong. If that's worth anything.'

Sakura smiles. 'Nah. Sorry, kiddo. Ain't worth nothin',' she says with a laugh, and then punches him on the arm.

Hotaka grabs her wrist. 'I'm serious, Sakura. What you've done is brave and strong and inspiring.' He steps closer. 'I think you're amazing.' He holds her gaze for a moment, but then a head pokes between them.

'Sorry to break up the love birds.' It's Osamu. He smooches Hotaka. 'Am I amazing too?'

They shove him away. 'What a goon!' Sakura growls.

'Aha! Sweet Juliet has recovered from her illness, I see.' Osamu turns to Hotaka. 'And what of Romeo? How dost thou fare, pray tell?'

Hotaka rolls his eyes. 'Oh, shut up!'

'Have it your way. As it happens, there's much more afoot in our fair town of Omori-wan than mere romance.'

'What are you talking about?'

'Oh, come on. You must have heard. Everyone is talking about it.'

Hotaka and Sakura stare blankly at Osamu.

'The seawall?' he prompts. 'The graffiti? Fall the Wall, Seawall Bad Call. It's great stuff.'

They shake their heads and shrug.

'Oh, forget it,' Osamu says and strides off.

Hotaka and Sakura cross the quadrangle in fits of laughter.

But in the car park they see two utility vehicles from the construction company responsible for the seawall, and stop at once. Both vehicles are plastered with graffiti.

'Whoa, Sakura!' he mutters. 'You really gave it to them.'

'No way!' Sakura snaps. 'We only did the concrete panels. *Nothing* else, I swear.' The colour drains from her face. 'I wonder—' she mutters, but suddenly turns and marches off. 'See you in class.'

The school bell rings as Hotaka secures his bike. On his way to the lockers he hears an announcement over the PA system.

'*There will be a special assembly first thing this morning. All students and teachers please proceed straight to the main assembly hall and fall into your class groups.*'

Hotaka is not sure he likes the sound of that.

'Shamed.'

Principal Hashimoto lets the word hang in the air like a noose. He stands centre stage, dark-suited, grim-faced, a tremble in his voice as he repeats the word.

'Shamed.'

Behind him sit two equally grim-faced men in dark suits. One is Mayor Nakano. The other is Mr Oshita, regional manager of the company building the seawall, Capitol Constructions. Their arms are folded. Behind them are the teachers. They sit very still.

'Our school has been shamed.'

Osamu nudges Hotaka. 'Told you it was big. Hashimoto looks like death warmed up.'

'Yeah,' Hotaka replies, glancing around. 'Have you seen Sakura?'

'Can't you stop thinking about her for one second? This is huge, man! We have been shamed!'

'*Your* school has been shamed,' the principal bellows. 'The night before last, at the harbourfront, public property was defaced with graffiti, machinery vandalised. Closed-circuit television reveals this to be the work of four young people, school age, faces masked by balaclavas.

We already know the identity of one. A security guard followed that person home, and to our great shame I must report that they attend this school. We have the student in question and they have admitted their guilt. They will be dealt with appropriately.'

Osamu chuckles. 'Maybe it's your girlfriend.'

'Shut it!' Hotaka snaps. 'She's not my girlfriend! Get that into your stupid head, will you?'

Osamu holds up his hands, don't-shoot mode. 'Sorreeee. *Joking.*'

'I'm just worried about her,' Hotaka mutters. 'She should be here.' Sakura has to be the one Principal Hashimoto is talking about. Is she up in his office?

'Don't worry,' Osamu says. 'She doesn't want to hear Hashimoto reading the riot act, that's all. Probably off tweeting somewhere.'

Hotaka hardly hears him. Or the principal, who is still talking as well.

'And what of the other three? We'll find you, rest assured. After all, the student we've already caught knows who you are.'

Hotaka cranes his neck, peering all around the hall, searching. Principal Hashimoto's voice grows louder, but all Hotaka catches are snippets. *Honour. Your school. Do the right thing. Give yourself up. End the shame. Disgrace.* He wishes the words would stop.

When the assembly eventually finishes Hotaka he races to the principal's office, reaching it just as Mr Hashimoto and the other men are closing the door. Shoving it wide open, Hotaka barges into the room.

# Twenty-six

**'Hotaka? What's going on?'** Mr Hashimoto demands.

'Where's Sakura? What have you done with her?'

'I've expelled her. I had no choice.'

'Yes, you did! You could've just suspended her at the most, until—'

'No, Hotaka. I decided that what she did demanded serious penalising.'

'What? She splattered some paint on a few ugly concrete panels.'

'And the machinery she vandalised,' the construction manager adds. 'Don't forget that.'

'Lies!' Hotaka glares at the manager. 'Sakura is no vandal, and she wouldn't let the others damage stuff.' He turns back to the principal. 'Please, I beg you, this is wrong. Expelling her will mean she loses her place at the Special Sendai High School.'

The mayor steps forward. 'Pity she didn't think of that before she committed the crime.'

Hotaka doesn't even acknowledge Mr Nakano. He keeps his attention on the principal.

'She won that position through hard work. You know she did. You praised her for it in assembly.'

Mr Hashimoto fidgets. 'This changes everything.'

'You're right it does. Expelling her will take that all away. You can't do it.'

'He can,' Mr Nakano insists. 'He is the principal. It's his decision and it's final. Now, I really have more important things to attend to.'

The mayor turns to leave, but Hotaka blocks his way.

'Hear me out, mayor.'

'How dare you?'

'I know what's going on. This is not the principal's decision at all; it's yours. You and Engineer Oshita are the ones calling the shots here.'

'Don't be ridiculous.'

'You want Sakura expelled to silence her. You're frightened her graffiti will set off an anti-seawall movement in town.'

'The boy's talking nonsense, Hashimoto. Discipline him, man!'

'You also said this was final. Wrong. This isn't the end at all; it's only the beginning. What Sakura has done will give the people in this town a voice they didn't even know they had. And you're not going to like what they say.'

Hotaka opens the door and turns to leave, but stops. 'By the way,' he says to Mr Hashimoto, 'I must tell you that I am one of those other so-called criminals who helped Sakura.'

'No, Hotaka. I don't believe you.'

'I was there the other night, sir. *I was there!* So you had better expel me as well.'

Hotaka slams the door on the grim-faced, dark-suited men.

Hotaka races down the hill from the school on his bike, searching for Sakura. He finds her sitting by the roadside, head in her hands. Dropping his bike, he rushes to her side. She looks up.

'What have I done? It's not me I'm worried about. It's my aunt and uncle. They'll be devastated. Expelled! I owe them so much. They took me in when I had nowhere to go. They bent over backwards to give me opportunities. They paid the tuition fees that helped me make it into Sendai. They're poor, and how do I repay them? By being expelled! They deserve so much more.'

'You studied hard, you passed those tests and won that place fair and square. It's yours.'

'Not anymore. I've thrown it away.'

'Not necessarily.'

'The mayor and that manager are talking criminal charges when we did not lay a finger on their machinery. Honest! I'll lose the position for sure if they take this any further.'

'Oh, this will definitely go further, Sakura, a lot further. But that's exactly what those guys don't want. They want to kill it now; hence all the threats. But you have right on your side, and unless I'm mistaken you're going to have a lot of people on your side as well; most of the town, I bet. In the end your uncle and aunt will be proud of you. I am already.'

'Thanks, but that's just wishful thinking. I should've thought before I acted. I've been really stupid.'

'Then so have I.'

'What do you mean?'

Hotaka tells Sakura what went on in the principal's office. She leaps up.

'You go right back there and tell them the truth. Now!'

'No way. This is too big to go back. Anyway, we won't be alone for long. This is a snowball. Small now, but it's only just started rolling. You wait.'

'I'm not sure I want to wait. Everything's so scary.'

'Don't worry, Sakura. I'll stand with you, whatever happens.'

'Thanks. That means a lot. It really does.'

Sakura gazes across the bay to the hills and beyond, as if searching for something.

'When I was little I had a special place I'd go if things got too much – a quiet place away from everyone. I'd go there to find myself again. It was a little garden in a valley not far from our house, so overgrown that you could easily miss it. A hidden garden. Whenever I sat in there I felt so safe.'

'Sounds beautiful.'

'It was. Probably still is. But I'll never know. I'm not allowed there anymore. No one is.'

'Why not?'

'It's poisoned. Radiation.'

'Fukushima?'

'Yes. Part of the Exclusion Zone. Everything was

144

poisoned: soil, flowers, crops, trees, animals, the air.' Sakura tenses. 'And people.'

'Your parents?'

Sakura nods. 'Farmers. Small-time, but it was everything, our wonderful way of life. Then suddenly it was over. No choice. Get out! They made us leave, the government officials, the military. Go! Barely time to grab anything. *The animals*, my father cried. *We feed them daily. They need us.* Go! Get out!

'He tried to return many times, but they always chased him away. It was forever, they said, fifty years at least. That drove my father mad. My mother tried to keep his spirit up, but then she was diagnosed with cancer. Terminal. That was the final straw. He left me a note, apologising. *We will only be a burden on you. It's for the best.* The best!?'

Hotaka can see that Sakura is fighting back her tears.

'How can that be for the best? For ages I blamed him. Then I blamed the radiation for stealing everything from me – my parents, my home. But I now know who the real thieves were – the politicians and the power company executives. The whole Fukushima Daiichi disaster was their fault, but they lied through their teeth to save their skins. They destroyed so many lives, but saved their own skins.'

Sakura's gaze returns to the harbour.

'And they're doing it again. Here. They're so big and powerful; they're our Godzilla, Hotaka, and they terrify me. That's why I wish I had somewhere like that hidden garden to go to again – even if only for a short while – somewhere to find my strength.'

Hotaka smiles. 'I have a place like that. Haven't been there for years.' He holds out his hand. 'Come on.'

# Twenty-seven

**They head to the harbour.** A small crowd is looking at the graffiti and talking excitedly.

'See what I mean?' Hotaka says as they pass. 'You're famous!'

'Quiet! Where are you taking me?'

'How about a deserted island?' Hotaka suggests, stepping onto the marina. 'Or, even better, a hidden cove?'

'Very funny.'

'I'm serious. Keep up.'

He goes straight to his uncle's boat-shed, drops his bike and enters. Uncle Yori is on a stool mending a lobster pot. He stands as soon as he sees Sakura and is about to say something, but Hotaka speaks first.

'Uncle, this is Sakura Tsukino.'

'Delighted to meet you.' Uncle Yori bows.

'She did the graffiti,' Hotaka adds.

Sakura glares at him. But Uncle Yori immediately claps his hands in delight.

'Then I am honoured as well,' he says. 'Deeply honoured. Well done, my dear.'

Sakura blushes. 'Thank you, sir. It's good to know someone cares.'

'People care, don't you worry. They just don't know how to express it...yet.' Uncle Yori takes a good look at Sakura, nods, then turns to Hotaka. 'I think Mayor Nakano is in for quite a shock.'

'I *know* he is, Uncle Yori. But right now I must ask a favour.'

'What is it?'

'I wondered if we could take out Jīchan's boat?'

'I told you before, the sabani is yours. Come, I'll help.'

Hotaka takes Sakura to a beach on the ocean side of the headland, only an hour from Omori-wan, but a world away. They cut across the bay and out into the open sea, then skirt the coast a short sail north to a tiny cove.

'You *were* serious,' Sakura says as they slide the sabani ashore. 'It really is a hidden cove.'

They walk up the beach and sit in the soft white sand.

'It's perfect,' Sakura sighs, lying back in the warm spring sun. Hotaka hears the dreaminess in her voice, and doesn't bother replying. He knows how exhausted she is, and lets her sleep. It's what she needs. Besides, he has plenty to keep himself busy. This place is full of memories.

He sits back and drifts into a kind of dreaminess himself. This is where he and Grandpa spent so much time together, and Hotaka can feel the old man's spirit, not in any particular place or thing, but everywhere – the rocks, the sand, the water, the breeze, the air – a soothing, peaceful presence.

Hotaka feels Takeshi's spirit here as well, having sensed him when he and Sakura arrived. He looks around, glancing across to the cliff they both used to leap from, and knows that Takeshi is somewhere near.

'Where are you, my friend?' he whispers.

Stillness descends. There's a breeze on the water further out, but here is an all-encompassing calm that transports Hotaka to somewhere that is everywhere. He hovers in an eerie, timeless silence.

Sakura suddenly stirs. She gives a little gasp and sits up, squinting at the sun.

'I drifted off.'

'You did, and for quite a while.' Hotaka smiles as the breeze joins them again. 'I've never seen you look so peaceful.'

'How long have we been here?'

'I'm not sure.' He checks. 'A couple of hours actually.'

'I slept that long?'

'I think I might have, too. You sure needed it, though, I know that much.'

Sakura stretches. 'Thanks for this. It's beautiful here.'

'I call it Grandpa's Beach. We used to come here all the time; fishing, swimming, diving.'

'What fun. You must teach me one day.'

'To dive?'

'No, to swim.'

'What? You can't swim?'

Sakura shakes her head.

'But how come?'

'We didn't live by the sea. There was no need.'

'But you've just been right out to sea, and you can't swim?'

'You're a good sailor. Your uncle said so.'

'But even the best sailors hit trouble. What if you'd been thrown into the water?'

'I'm wearing a life jacket, duh.'

'I know, but—'

'But, but, but. You sound like a busted motorboat. Lose the buts. They just get in the way.'

Hotaka stands. 'What did you say?'

A dizziness grips him. His eyes creep across the beach and over a stretch of deep water to the base of the cliff. There's no stopping them.

'Are you okay?' Sakura asks.

He can't reply. His eyes are already climbing the cliff. Higher.

'Did I say something wrong?'

Higher. Only when they reach the top do they stop. He swallows hard.

*Two boys stare into the sea, toes poking over the edge.*

*'Ready?' the taller one whispers.*

*The smaller boy swallows hard.*

*'We agreed. Today is the day. The big leap.'*

*'I know, but…'*

*'Forget the buts, Hotaka. Buts get in the way of everything.'*

'I can't,' Hotaka whispers.

'What is it? Are you okay?' Sakura is standing beside him, a steadying hand on his arm.

Hotaka shudders, still uneasy. 'We should go.'

'Not until you tell me what that was about.'

'All right. On the way.'

They walk to the boat. Sakura climbs aboard while Hotaka checks the ropes and sails, then pushes off. A gust catches them and they're soon skimming out to sea. At a safe distance from the shore, Hotaka turns the boat and points towards the cliff.

'I used to jump from there.'

'Right up there?'

'Not quite. From that halfway ledge. I wanted to go from the top, but I couldn't.'

'I'm not surprised. It's so high!'

'Yes, but it was always my dream.'

'Why?'

'To be like Takeshi.'

'Takeshi?'

'My best friend. My hero. He was like a brother.'

'I get it. He jumped from the top.'

'No. He *dived*.'

'Impossible.'

'He did. I would've been happy to just jump like a frightened frog, but I couldn't even do that. All through summer he'd urge me on. A few times I came close, only to pull out, always with some lame excuse – *but this, but that*. Those freakin' buts!'

A strong gust hits them and the boat rocks as though impatient. Hotaka steadies it, easing the sheets.

'The last time we came here, Takeshi lost his patience. And do you know what he said?' Hotaka turns to Sakura.

'What you said. *Forget the buts. They get in the way of everything.* When you said those words on the beach, it was as if Takeshi was talking *through* you.'

'So where is Takeshi now?'

'Lost. The wave.' Hotaka finds it difficult to speak. 'We were rescuing people. Takeshi kept going back. We were exhausted, but Takeshi wouldn't stop.' He takes a deep breath. 'And then he was gone.'

Sakura frowns. 'Except he hasn't gone, has he? He's still with you. Isn't he?'

'If only…' Hotaka can't finish. *If only I, if only he, if only we could find peace.*

He bears the boat away from the wind and tightens the sheets. They sail off, each wrapped in their own thoughts. He glances back once, but Sakura keeps her gaze on the cliff.

They continue down the coast in silence. It's a fast ride, for the on-shore breeze is strong. Only after they leave the open sea and are halfway across the bay does Sakura speak.

'I'm still exhausted, you know?' she says.

'Hardly surprising. I bet you've barely slept in the last two days.'

She yawns. 'When I get back I'm going to crash big-time.'

'No, you aren't.'

'Why not?'

Hotaka nods towards the marina.

Sakura turns and gasps.

# Twenty-eight

**A large crowd is gathered** at the harbourfront, spilling onto the marina.

'What a welcome,' Hotaka says. 'There's a TV crew.'

Sakura groans. 'I don't think I can face this.'

'You have to.'

'But I'm exhausted. I won't know what to say.'

'You, lost for words?' Hotaka holds up a clenched fist. 'You can do it.'

'Sure, easy as jumping off a cliff.'

'Hey, that was mean!'

Uncle Yori is waiting. He's been able to close the gate into his wharf, keeping the crowd out. As Hotaka and Sakura pull alongside, Osamu steps from the boat-shed.

'I couldn't keep him out,' Uncle Yori explains. 'He said you need him.'

'And you do,' Osamu adds.

Sakura groans. 'Like a hole in the head.'

'You guys have been gone for ages. What have you been doing?'

'What's it matter?' Sakura snaps as she clambers off the boat.

'What's it matter? See the crowd? Several hundred people here to see you, and you ask what's it matter? This could be bigger than Godzilla. While you've been on the high seas, a TV crew and newspaper reporters from Sendai have shown up, plus there's a team flying up from Tokyo as we speak! And you ask—'

'Okay, got the picture.' Sakura steadies herself against the boat-shed. 'I'll handle it.'

'No, you won't. You're a mess. Those creeps will eat you. They'll put words in your mouth and have you saying all the wrong things. You need a media manager, someone to keep those dogs at bay. And who better than…moi!'

'Are you kidding?'

'Trust me. I know what I'm talking about.'

'You *aren't* kidding. I'm outa here!' Sakura starts to walk away, but Osamu stops her.

'At least hear me out. Please.'

Sakura stops and turns back to him. 'Go on, then. I'm listening.'

'First off, it's not easy for me to say this; after all, probably the one thing we both agree on is that we disagree a lot.'

Sakura nods. 'True.'

'But I honestly think that what you've done is incredibly brave. You've stood up and said something that many in this town might have thought but haven't had the guts to say. In doing so you've become a voice for many, an important voice. You've also started a fight that could radically change this town. I feel honoured to call you my friend.'

Sakura's jaw drops. 'Oh my god! Am I hearing things?'

'Please don't make fun of me. I mean what I say.'

'I'm not making fun of you. I just didn't expect this.' Sakura reaches out to Osamu. 'Thanks.'

'There's more. This won't be an easy fight. There are big forces out there who want to squash you, and have the means to do it. How you handle the next part of this fight will be crucial. Do the wrong thing and you'll lose before you know it. I think I know how you can win, but you'll need to do what I say. Am I in?'

Sakura throws a questioning glance at Hotaka.

'What he says makes sense,' Hotaka replies, and then adds with a grin: 'For once. Maybe you should give him a chance.'

'Okay,' she says. 'You're in. So what's our plan of attack for the media? I have to front them.'

'No, let them come to you. You call the shots. You have to own this story. We must have those media grubs telling *your* story, not theirs or anyone else's.'

'Good point,' Sakura says. 'But how do we make that happen?'

Osamu claps his hands together, businesslike. 'You stay exactly where you are. I go to the media and explain that due to the huge stress you've been put under by the school, local government and the Shonkyshow Construction Co, you're exhausted and distressed. Despite this you will speak to them. But only for a short time; you really do need to recuperate. I'll explain that a fuller interview will be possible tomorrow.'

'Provided they behave,' Hotaka adds.

'Exactly! And Sakura will be the judge of that. Misbehave, and they don't get a second go. And if at any time you feel bullied or threatened, give your minder a nod.' Osamu points to Hotaka's uncle. 'He'll expel them on the spot. You cool with that, Captain Yori?'

'Absolutely,' Uncle Yori replies with a smile. He's enjoying this.

'I'd also appreciate it, Captain, if you'd come to the gate with me. Those media dogs can get snappy.' Osamu turns to Sakura. 'You okay? Ready for the show?'

'As ready as I'll ever be. Open those flood gates.'

Osamu nods to Hotaka and his uncle, and they head off.

'So what have you got lined up for me?' Hotaka asks as they walk.

'Plenty. You see, a lot has happened since this morning. Principal Hashimoto is tearing his hair out.'

'How come?'

'Remember how he said at assembly that there were three others in this with Sakura? Once word got out about you putting up your hand, at least twenty others have done the same. Even your kendo pal has joined the team, plus a few of his mates.' Osamu shakes his head. 'This is going to get big and almost certainly nasty. Sakura has to be careful.' Osamu stops and pulls Hotaka closer. 'She can't go home tonight. The media will find out where she lives and pester her nonstop.'

'She can stay at my place.'

'I hoped you'd say that.' Osamu hands Hotaka a piece of paper. 'When you're clear of here, call my cousin. He's come to Omori-wan from Kyoto for work. Tell him to bring his car around to Wharf 21. Go there and wait for him.'

'Wharf 21? That's way down the other end of the marina. How will Sakura get there?'

'Your uncle has that sorted.'

Hotaka slaps Osamu on the back. 'You've really thought this through, bud. Good work.'

'I hope so,' Osamu replies. 'These dudes can be devious.'

They go on to the gate. As they near it the media people call out.

'The graffiti girl,' a TV reporter yells. 'We want to talk to the graffiti girl.'

'Yeah,' another calls out. 'Where is she?'

Uncle Yori steps forward. 'Settle down,' he shouts. 'All of you. The girl you want is Miss Sakura Tsukino. Refer to her properly and we might just let you in for a little chat.'

A newspaper reporter responds quickly. 'Would it be possible to interview Miss Tsukino please?'

'Certainly, sir,' Uncle Yori replies. 'See what manners do.' He unlocks the gate, keeping a firm grip on it, and directs Hotaka through. 'Let this guy out first,' he shouts. 'And don't bother pestering him. He's not part of this thing at all.'

Hotaka squeezes through the gate and pushes past the

media people, smiling to himself as he hears his uncle laying down the law.

'Listen up, everyone. A few ground rules before anyone gets in.'

# Twenty-nine

**'This is not about me.'**

Sakura's face fills the screen, her gaze unflinching. It's the late news, and Hotaka is with his mother and Uncle Yori. He wonders what Sakura will think when she sees this in the morning. She's sound asleep right now, having gone to bed as soon as she arrived at Hotaka's house. She has good reason to feel pleased with herself, he decides as he watches.

*'I'm just a voice for all the people who need to be heard by the politicians and so-called decision-makers who are throwing away our money on crazy projects like this seawall, money that should be used to make those people's lives liveable.'*

Hotaka can hardly believe that the girl on the screen is the same one he left in the boat-shed that afternoon. That girl was on the point of collapse. This one is fired up and fierce.

*'I'm a voice for the little people, those living in squalor almost three years after being promised recovery. A voice for those struggling to rebuild their lives with nothing but hollow*

*words. And yes, a voice for the young, for my generation –
because we are the ones who will have to pay for the insane
spendathon that's going on in the name of recovery. Shame!'*

'About time somebody said it,' Uncle Yori mutters.
'She's good.'

The camera cuts to the reporter, the seawall and
graffiti visible in the distance.

'*That was Sakura Tsukino, the young girl whipping up
a tsunami of trouble in the normally quiet Tōhoku town of
Omori-wan. Social campaigner or teenage troublemaker?
Voice for the voiceless or vicious vandal? One highly respected
member of this community, Mayor Nakano, is in no doubt.*'

The camera moves to Mayor Nakano. Several
vehicles can be seen behind him, some owned by Capitol
Constructions, others by the council. All have been
sprayed with graffiti, and three are seriously damaged
with dents and broken windows.

'*The graffiti is ugly and offensive,*' the mayor says. '*It'll
also be expensive to remove. But the really unacceptable part
is the wilful wrecking of public and commercial property.*'

The camera zooms in on the most damaged vehicle.

'*This is not just a silly prank by some kids. It's a crime.
As mayor of this normally law-abiding town, I have no choice
but to involve the police.*'

Hotaka leaps up. 'Liar!'

The reporter steps in front of the vehicle. '*We sought
further comment from Miss Tsukino, but our sources say she
has since gone into hiding.*' The camera pulls back for a
wide-angle view of the marina and bay as the reporter
signs off. '*Ichiro Kimura for Late Night News.*'

'I don't believe it,' Hotaka hisses angrily, and flicks off the television after saving the interview. 'They've twisted things. Sakura assured me she only did the seawall graffiti, nothing else. Neither she nor any of the others touched those vehicles. It's a frame-up.'

His phone buzzes with a text message. He glances at it.

'Osamu again?' his mother asks.

Hotaka nods and reads the message aloud. '*Creeps! They chopped Sakura to bits, edited out heaps.*'

'They sure did,' Uncle Yori agrees. 'She said a lot more, all of it good. They cut at least half out.'

Hotaka reads on. '*Then they buried her in the late news. But that mayor was the worst. Total liar!*'

'Of course he is.' Uncle Yori snickers. 'It wouldn't be the first time Nakano has smeared others with his own dirt. How do you think he got where he is? Bribes, black-mail, deals with the yakuza, lying and cheating – that creep is so bent he can't even lie straight in bed.'

'It's so wrong.'

'Sure, but what do you do about it?'

As Hotaka fumes for an answer, another text comes through from Osamu. He glances at his phone and smiles.

'We take him on, Uncle. That's what we do. We expose him.'

'That's what I like to hear,' Uncle Yori says as he stands to go. 'But we'll need to be careful,' he adds. 'They play rough.'

Once Uncle Yori has driven off, Hotaka turns to his mother.

'I worry so much for Sakura. The mayor and his lot want to kill her message at any cost.'

'Don't worry, Sakura is impressive. That news item might have been brief and kept until late, but more will have seen it than you realise. And it will definitely have made them sit up and think.'

'I hope you're right. She's sure made me sit up and think.'

'I can see that, Hotaka. Which is why you'd better go to bed now and *stop* thinking, before you collapse like Sakura.'

Hotaka does go to bed, but he can't stop thinking. He pulls out his phone and calls Osamu.

'When you said we take on the mayor, what did you mean?'

'Stuff's all over Facebook and Twitter. And three popular current-affairs blogs – TruNewz, Skoopskape and AzitiZ – all want to run Sakura's full TV interview, which I videoed on my phone. I'll also get it up on YouTube. That will get *all* the facts out there, rather than the chopped-back version those TV goons spewed up.'

'Hey, you really *have* been busy.'

'That's just the beginning. Like I said, we have to own this. That TV interview shows what happens when we don't. So for tomorrow I've lined up some kids to do on-site interviews with people at the harbourfront; they'll be beamed on TruNewz and the other blogs. There'll also be a door-knock. I'm sure most people are against the seawall, but we must ram home the message loud and clear. And part of that is keeping Sakura in the public eye as well.'

'Yeah, but she wants this to be about the issue, not about her. She doesn't want to be the star.'

'She's already the star. Without her, the anti-seawall song has no singer. We have to keep her up front in people's minds. Trust me, I know what I'm talking about.'

'Okay, but be careful. She's not as tough as you think. Push her too hard and you might lose her. Trust me, Osamu, I know what I'm talking about, too.'

'That's why we need you, Romeo. Therefore art thou! It's your job to make sure we don't lose her. Sweet dreams.'

# Thirty

**A chill grips Hotaka as** he stares into the early morning mist from his bedroom window. A large grey rat dangles from the verandah post by a black and yellow cord. It slowly rotates until it is facing him. The animal pauses, its lifeless eyes locked onto him. He's repulsed by how big and bulging they are but can't look away. Eventually the rat starts turning back, and the eyes move with it.

*Of course!* It's a warning. Hotaka rushes onto the verandah to get rid of the thing before his mother or Sakura sees it. He grabs the cord and rips the creature down, then runs through the garden and across the road to hurl it into the bushes. He stands for a while, letting his pounding heart settle before returning to the house.

He washes his hands, suddenly feeling very vulnerable. His life, his security, has been invaded as though it means nothing. Someone – more than one? – came to his house during the night and hung that rat outside his bedroom window. *This could happen to you!*

His window? How did they know it was his bedroom?

Maybe the rat wasn't meant for him? Maybe it was for Sakura.

Hotaka spins round and races through the house to Sakura's room. But he skids to a stop at her door. If she's there he mustn't wake her. If? Of course she's there, he tells himself. What's all this worry? What's he doing here? Hotaka steps back and very nearly walks away, but then steadies himself and quietly slides the door open.

He peers into the darkness. Unable to make out anything clearly, he tiptoes across the tatami floor to the futon. All he can see is a tangle of bedclothes, so he kneels and leans closer. Sakura is completely wrapped in the quilt, her face pearly pale. Hotaka sighs with relief, the tension easing from his body.

Sakura sleeps until midday. Hotaka lets her bathe, eat breakfast, and watch her televised interview before texting Osamu that she's awake – his mother's orders. Osamu has already messaged three times and called twice, keen to get the show on the road. He arrives almost as soon as Hotaka texts.

'You must've been waiting around the corner,' Hotaka says at the front door.

'I was,' Osamu replies. 'There's too much to do and too little time. Is she ready?'

'She should be.' Hotaka beckons him in.

'Should be?' Osamu groans, kicks off his shoes and pulls on some slippers. 'We could lose some bigs scoops if we don't hurry.'

'Such as?' Hotaka asks as they walk along the rōka.

'For starters, stacks of kids have skipped school and are taking selfies in front of the seawall, some even adding graffiti themselves. They want Sakura in their pics as well. Think of all the publicity! But it has to happen before the graffiti gets painted over. Like ASAP!'

Hotaka pauses at the fusuma doors into the dining room. There's muted laughter on the other side. He taps and gently slides open the doors.

Sakura sits on the zabuton in the middle of the room, listening closely to Hotaka's mother who kneels opposite, talking quietly. Hotaka catches some words.

'He was only three at the time.'

'Three!' Sakura gasps, pressing her hand to her mouth. 'That's incredible, Yamato-san.'

Hotaka clears his throat. They turn, stare at him, and burst out laughing.

'Are you telling stories about me, Okāsan?'

'Who said we're talking about you?' His mother turns back to Sakura. 'Typical male. They think we have nothing better to do than talk about them.'

Osamu steps forward and bows. 'Hello, Yamato-san.'

'Osamu. Good to see you, but I fear you've come to take our guest away. What a pity. She's a delight.'

'Yes, Yamato-san, I'm afraid we must get started,' Osamu replies. 'There is a great deal to do. We have to drum up as much support as we can for Sakura in her fight against the seawall.'

'Support?' Sakura scoffs. 'What do you think we've been doing? Please, Yamato-san, would you be kind enough to enlighten the boy?'

165

'It's nothing, really. But there are some spare funds from one of our campaigns for the disadvantaged in Omori-wan. I called the committee members last night and they agreed that the money should go into your anti-seawall campaign. I hope you can make good use of it.'

'Wonderful,' Osamu says. 'Thank you so much. We will make very good use of it!'

'I'd better not keep you away from the fight, then. Off you go. I'll be there. And good luck.'

'I want you all to do some serious thinking.'

Sakura stands in front of the three graffiti-covered concrete panels, addressing a crowd of over five hundred people, many around her age.

'When finished, this wall will have cost at least 400 million yen. *At least!* Add all the walls to be built along the Tōhoku coast, and the cost will be astronomical! And it's all money that you will have to pay back in the years to come. *You!*'

She shouts the last word, then waves her arms over the whole crowd, and points directly at some younger ones.

'Our generation will still be paying off this wall when we're old! *Think about that!* It's a terrible thought, but it's made even worse by the fact that this wall will not even do the job it is meant to do. All that money for nothing! How stupid is that?'

Sakura pauses, allowing her words to sink in.

'Now think about this. For a small part of that wall's cost, we could build good housing for everyone who's been living down here in terrible conditions for nearly three years. For a fraction of what that monster will cost, these people could get their lives back on track. Isn't that what recovery *really* should be about?'

Sakura glares at the seawall panels.

'But of course, those in power think recovery means more and more concrete blocks. Why? Because pouring cement is far easier than repairing lives. So that's what our politicians and decision-makers do: they take the easy road. They leave all those damaged lives down here – out of sight, out of mind – to rot. And instead they build a wall. A *wall*!'

She screams the word this time, and then is silent. Hotaka is close enough to see that she is in fact overcome by emotion.

'What a horrible thought,' she eventually continues. 'All those poor people trapped inside a faulty concrete fortress, a kind of prison, hearing the ocean but unable to see it. That is criminal. That thought makes me want to weep.' She bows her head.

There's complete stillness when Sakura finishes; people are stunned. A moment later they break into applause.

'She's good, eh?' Osamu joins Hotaka in clapping wildly. He's been busy instructing a team of helpers, making sure they record everything from different angles. 'And guess what? Hashimoto is in the audience!'

'Scowling, I bet.'

'No. Our esteemed principal was listening intently. Our princess is a born politician.'

'True, but don't tell her that – or call her a princess,' Hotaka warns. 'She'll eat you.'

Osamu laughs. 'She was awesome. Had the crowd captivated, young and old. Look at all the phones and cameras out now, clicking and snapping away. Gotta love it, pal; this will definitely spiral viral.'

Hotaka agrees; Sakura was fantastic. But he can't enjoy the moment like Osamu. He's unable to relax because he can't get that strangled rat out of his head. Ever since this morning he's been thinking about the creature. Right through Sakura's speech he couldn't stop searching faces, assessing people, wondering. Who did it? Would they be here now?

He stares out at the crowd, and although he knows that most people support Sakura, all he can see are those who don't. Like the construction workers, with their hard hats and angry faces. Or the bunch of local officials and construction company executives in dark suits muttering among themselves, their black four-wheel drives in the background with scowling minders. And then there are the three thugs standing alone, arms folded; he's never seen them before in Omori-wan, and doesn't like the look of them. Could they be yakuza?

Hotaka decides he has to talk to someone about his concerns. He doesn't want to worry Osamu and Sakura, or his mother. Besides, they wouldn't know what to do any more than he would. Uncle Yori is the only one.

'Listen,' he says to Osamu. 'I just remembered

something important. I told my uncle I'd call in on him this morning. He'll be wondering why I didn't show up. I'd better rush down there now. You okay here?'

'No worries. This show is running itself. Just look at that queue for selfies with Sakura! We'll need ages to milk this. Catch you at the boat-shed.'

'Keep a close eye on Sakura, won't you,' Hotaka says as he walks off.

# Thirty-one

'A rat?'

Uncle Yori looks up from the net he's repairing. He's sitting on the deck of his trawler, working in the warm sun.

'I got a rat too. Hanging from the mast this morning. I tossed it into the water. Kept the rope, though.' He digs in his pocket and pulls out a length of cord.

'It's the same as mine,' Hotaka says. 'Black and yellow.'

'Of course. Black for evil and misfortune. Yellow for cowardice. The message: we're cowardly rats who will meet with evil misfortune if we don't behave.'

'Who do you reckon did it?'

'Low-life crims would've done the deed, but the mayor is definitely behind it, and maybe the local head of Capitol Constructions. The company itself is clean but that local guy is in with the yakuza and as corrupt as they come. Trouble is, we'd never pin anything on those two unless we caught the crooks and made them squeal. We just have to wear this and watch our backs. Or our necks, actually.'

'So you think they'll do more?'

'The rat's just a warning. They could make life very nasty for us. They've already given me a taste of what to expect.'

'What do you mean?'

'Well, they've damaged my nets for a start.' Uncle Yori holds up the one he's repairing, and nods at another two nearby. 'These will take days to fix. They also put a hole in my runabout. And—' He frowns as though not wanting to go on, then puts down the net and stands. 'See for yourself.'

As Hotaka follows his uncle into the boat-shed he has a nasty feeling that he knows what he's about to see. Even so, he's not fully prepared. His grandfather's boat has been smashed – mast and boom broken, and several panels hopelessly splintered. He wants to rage in anger, but can only manage a stifled cry of anguish.

Uncle Yori tries his best to comfort Hotaka. 'At least you got to sail her before they did this.'

'I'm so sorry, Uncle Yori.'

'So am I.'

'You don't have to get involved in any of this. It's not your problem, and these guys could make things awful for you.'

'Hey, I rode out the 3/11 tsunami. I took on monster waves and spent days at sea tossed about like a cork. Whatever these guys throw at me could never be that bad.'

'But look what they've done.' Hotaka stares at the wrecked sabani. 'All that work.'

'Oh, that's not important. She can be repaired. No, it's the insult that upsets me. Wrecking that boat is an insult to your jīchan. He did so much for this town. He helped others less fortunate. He helped fishermen and townsfolk in all sorts of ways. People loved him and his little sabani. Omori-wan's old man of the sea, they called him.'

Uncle Yori grits his teeth, struggling to control his anger.

'What those dogs have done here is unbelievably insulting to his memory.' He picks up part of the broken rudder arm and whacks it into the palm of his other hand. 'But what they've done is also super stupid. They've made some real enemies. A few of my friends know about this, and their feelers are out for who did it. If they discover the culprits, there'll be no escape. Smashing that boat could be the biggest mistake those guys ever made.'

He strikes the piece of rudder arm hard into his hand again, then returns it to the boat.

'Ahoy there!' The shout comes from the far end of the wharf. 'Anyone on board?'

'That's Osamu,' Hotaka says. 'We agreed to meet here. I hope you don't mind.'

'Of course not.' His uncle turns away from the little boat. 'But let's not mention any of this, eh?'

Hotaka closes the door on the back room, and they walk through the shed to the wharf, where Osamu and Sakura are waiting. Uncle Yori greets them.

'Hotaka tells me you had a real victory today,' he says.

'You bet we did,' Osamu replies. 'We have just kicked arse big-time!' Sakura is standing back, but Osamu grabs her wrist, pulls her forward and holds up her arm like a boxer who's won a fight. 'And this is the biggest arse-kicker of all!'

Sakura grimaces and pulls her arm down. Hotaka can feel the tension between his friends, and tries to smooth things over.

'I didn't think you'd be here for ages,' he says to Sakura. 'You must have got through the selfies at record speed. The queue was huge when I left.'

She shrugs. 'There was a bit of trouble, actually.'

'Trouble?'

Osamu butts in. 'Some construction workers crashed the party. Said they'd come to clean the wall.'

'You mean get rid of the graffiti?'

'Yep. They had a big spray unit to paint over the lot.'

'And did they?'

'We didn't hang around to see,' Sakura says. 'I wanted to, but Osamu said we should leave.'

'People started yelling,' Osamu says. 'Tempers were rising. I could see it getting out of hand. The construction guys wanted to stir up a fight, bang some heads.'

'That's not the only reason,' Sakura mutters.

'Okay. I also thought it'd be bad for Sakura's image if she was caught up in violent stuff.'

'My image?' Sakura shakes her head. 'I'm not a rock star.'

'You are to many of those people. You said it yourself – you're their voice.'

Hotaka sees Sakura's jaw tighten and her eyes flare. Knowing she could explode at any moment, he moves quickly.

'Rock star, huh?' he says, reaching out and touching her arm reassuringly. 'Can I have your autograph?' he adds with a take-it-easy smile.

But it's too little too late. Sakura pulls away and points at Osamu.

'He's impossible!' she yells. 'He's a freak.'

'Sure,' Hotaka replies. 'But he's our impossible freak. And his heart is in the right place.'

'I know that.'

'And you have to admit that he's really got this whole issue right out there in the public eye.'

'I know that too.'

'Without his full-on social media push, this might not have—'

'Okay! Enough of the Osamu Fujita Fan Club. I know all that. And I'm grateful. But he's still impossible.'

'So what's new?'

'I've had enough. That's what's new. I can't go on. Not like this.'

'What!' Osamu shouts. 'You're crazy.'

'No. You're crazy. You've gone mad with this seawall thing.'

'Hey, it's just how I am when I take something on board. You know that, Sakura.'

'You haven't just taken this on board; you've taken over the whole ship.'

'That's how I am when I run with something.'

'You're more than running with this; you're stealing the race. And I hate it. You've morphed into some kind of monster salesman who thinks his mission is to sell me on social media. I'm not for sale. You're turning this into a weird marketing exercise, hanging it on crappy airhead stuff like image and trending tweets and pins and how many likes you get and…aaarrrrr!' Sakura shakes both fists at the sky. 'That's not what this should be about.'

'Calm down,' Osamu pleads. 'This was always going to be bigger than you, Sakura.'

'I know that. But you're making this *about* me. That's totally against what I believe, and to be honest, I just can't take any more.'

'You have to.'

'No I don't.' Sakura glares at Osamu. 'And I won't!'

A tense silence wraps around the teenagers, the atmosphere charged with anger and defiance. Hotaka cannot believe it. Disaster is staring them in the face unless something can be done. He sees his uncle standing in the background, and suddenly has an idea.

'Uncle,' he cries. 'Help us, please. This is too important to lose.'

Uncle Yori walks over to Osamu and puts his arm around his shoulder. He draws him across to Sakura, placing his other arm around her shoulder. Then he nods to Hotaka to join them.

'You kids are amazing,' he says as they stand in a huddle. 'You've got fire in your guts like I've never seen before. It all started with you, Sakura, and that's where the main flame still burns strongest. But you passed it to Hotaka, then Osamu, and that flame has grown beyond all expectations. It now burns in the people of Omori-wan. I bet Mayor Nakano is beside himself right now, because the fire you three have started looks unstoppable.'

The big fisherman folds his arms and shakes his head.

'Except it isn't unstoppable. As huge as it might be, this fire could be extinguished in a blink by one silly little thing: by what you guys are doing right now – fighting among yourselves. Keep it up and you'll burn each other out. Mayor Nakano will be the winner, Omori-wan and all of us the losers. Like my nephew says, you'll lose everything you've fought so hard for.'

Uncle Yori steps back a little.

'It's up to you guys.' He stares at Osamu first, then at Sakura, and finally Hotaka. He gives his nephew an almost imperceptible nod.

Hotaka knows what to do. He turns to Osamu. 'Well? What do you say?'

Osamu immediately offers his hand to Sakura. 'I'm sorry. I didn't mean to get out of control. I'll try my hardest not to let it happen again, I promise. We can't let that flame die.'

Sakura slaps his hand away, but then grabs him by the shirt, pulls him closer and gives him a hug.

'Thanks,' she says, the emotion unmistakable in her voice. 'You big goon.'

Hotaka throws his arms around his friends. 'Phew! I'm glad that's over.' He calls to his uncle. 'Arigatō gozaimasu! You're a legend.'

'No,' Uncle Yori replies. 'You guys are the legends. Because all that out there is what you're fighting for.' He waves his arm in a broad sweep of the hills, the bay, the ocean. 'The right to have that as part of your life – along

176

with all the other faces and moods of Nature, good and bad.'

The sun is reluctantly releasing its grip on the day, the light slowly sighing out of sight behind the hills, leaving the bay in a play of delicately changing hues. The scene holds them entranced.

But then Sakura suddenly shouts.

'Oh my god!' she cries. 'I forgot. I promised my aunt I'd call in on her.' She glances hopefully at the boys. 'I could do with some moral support, if you don't mind.'

'Lead on,' Osamu says. 'We'll be right behind.'

# Thirty-two

'**I am so sorry, Aunty.**'

'You mustn't be, Sakura.'

'But it's all my fault. I've been stupid and selfish. Believe me, I would never have done this if I'd known the trouble I would end up causing you and Uncle Hideo. I just didn't think.'

'Nonsense, my child. You are not causing us any trouble whatsoever. The boss at Capitol Constructions and his cronies are the troublemakers. Plus the mayor, of course.'

Sakura is sitting at the kitchen table with her Aunt Azumi; Hotaka and Osamu are there too. She's been crying over some bad news: her Uncle Hideo has had his work hours halved. More than that, the hours he's been given are all late-night shifts, the times no one wants. Worst of all, there's talk he could lose his job completely.

'It's all the Engineer Oshita's doing,' Sakura's aunt continues. 'To silence you. He knows that what you say is true. You've shown people that they can stand up for their rights. For that reason alone, we must not let him succeed.'

'Uncle Hideo could lose his job completely.'

'True. But he says it's horrible working there anyway. Oshita is targeting him nonstop: underpaying, over-working, cheating whenever he can. Your uncle nearly didn't go to work tonight. Said he couldn't care less if he lost his job.'

'That may be so, but you need the money. How would you survive without it?'

'We'd manage. We've struggled before. Perhaps I'll get a job.'

'You know that's not on, what with your arthritis the way it is.'

'Nonsense. The doctor says—'

'Stop pretending, Aunt Azumi. I can see that you're worried sick. I saw it when I walked in the door. I can see fear in your eyes right now. Try as you might, you can't hide that from me.'

Sakura's aunt closes her eyes and holds her hand to her mouth. 'I am worried, yes; I won't deny it. Very worried. But it's not to do with Uncle Hideo's job or the money. That's nothing compared to—' A shadow seems to pass over Aunt Azumi's face, and the blood drains from her cheeks.

'Compared to what, Aunty?'

'Something else has happened that is far more serious.'

'What? Tell me.'

'Look, it might be nothing. Maybe just a joke in bad taste.'

'*Tell me!*'

Hotaka feels certain that he knows what Sakura's aunt is talking about. 'Was it a rat?'

Aunt Azumi nods in astonishment.

'And was it hanging from the front door?' Hotaka continues. 'Or the verandah?'

'The gate,' Aunt Azumi replies.

'Black and yellow cord?'

'How did you know?'

'My uncle found one hanging from the mast of his trawler. I got one too.'

'And me.' Osamu leans forward. 'Someone is trying to frighten us.'

'Could someone please explain?' Sakura exclaims.

Osamu pulls out his phone. 'This is what we're talking about.' He shows her a photo of a strangled rat. 'We've all received one.'

'All dangling from the same type of cord,' Hotaka adds. 'Uncle Yori says they're a warning. *Back off or else.*'

'Or else what?' Sakura asks.

'Use your imagination,' Osamu replies, pretending to choke himself.

'That's why I'm so worried,' Aunt Azumi says. 'For you, Sakura, not for me and Uncle Hideo. I'm worried for your safety.'

'Well, don't be. That's exactly what they want.'

'I know, but these people can be ruthless.'

'I'm sure they can. But we can throw their tactics back in their face. Do you still have the rat, Aunt Azumi?'

'It's in the garbage bin.'

'Good. Can one of you boys fetch it, please?'

Osamu stands. 'What's the idea, Sakura?'

'Put on your lipstick, Ossy darling; we are going to post some rat selfies. Construction Giant Threatens School Kids. Graffiti Artists Intimidated. Rat Tactics in Seawall War.'

'Now you're talking! I'll go grab that rat.'

But before he even moves, a brick smashes through the kitchen window.

Aunt Azumi screams. She grabs her walking stick, hobbles to the window and flings it open.

The others rush to her side. Three dark figures – their faces hidden by balaclavas – are trampling Aunt Azumi's garden, hacking at her flowers with thick bamboo rods like the shinai used in kendo.

'Come on,' Hotaka yells, clambering through the window.

'You're mad,' Osamu shouts, but then shrugs. 'What the heck. You only die once.' He tosses his phone to Sakura. 'Record!' he tells her, and follows Hotaka.

Sakura flings the phone to her aunt. 'Get everything you can, Aunt Azumi,' she says and leaps through the window as well. 'Everything!'

'Wait!' Aunt Azumi cries. 'Use this.' She throws her walking stick to Sakura. 'And go for the one on his own over there with his back to us. Hit him hard and you'll knock him out.' Sakura heads for the far side of the garden.

The other two thugs laugh when they see the teenagers tumble out the window.

'This'll be fun,' the smallest one sneers, picking on Hotaka. 'Let me at him.'

'All yours,' his mate replies.

Hotaka is leapt upon before he even gains his balance. Solid and thickset, the guy hacks at him with his bamboo rod. Hotaka manages to drop and roll out of the way, grabbing a garden stake to fend off the next blow, and scrambles to his feet, trying to remember his kendo lessons. He lashes out with the stake and almost collects his opponent's face. This takes the thug by surprise and he stumbles backwards. Hotaka seizes the chance and springs forward, lunging at the guy's neck, but his thrust is knocked out of the way when the other man intervenes.

'Looks like this one thinks he knows a thing or two. Let's teach him a lesson.'

He hooks his bamboo cane under Hotaka's stake and flicks it from his hands, flinging it high into the air, then delivers a blow to Hotaka's ribs that makes him yelp in agony and collapse to his knees. The pain brings tears to his eyes. He peers up through the blur to see that both men are about to bring their rods down on him and lifts his arms to protect his head, preparing for the worst.

But before the pair can strike, Osamu hurls himself at them in a wild tackle that sends both men tumbling sideways. The smaller thug drops his rod in the fall, and in a mad scramble Osamu grabs the cane and tosses it to Hotaka.

'Kill 'em, Kendo Kid!' he manages to shout before being swamped by a torrent of punches.

While this is happening, Sakura attacks the biggest

intruder with her aunt's walking stick, aiming for his head. But he moves at the last moment and she misses, cracking him across the neck and shoulders. He roars and spins around. She hits out again, but he blocks the blow, pushing her over and knocking her face-first to the ground. Then he rips the walking stick from her and snaps it in half.

As Sakura struggles to get up, he rams his boot into her back, pinning her to the spot.

'Is this the one?' he grunts to his buddies, who are untangling themselves from Osamu.

'Yeah,' the smaller one yells. 'Shut her up for good – that's what they said.'

'Too easy,' the big guy growls, and with his bamboo rod gripped in both hands, he raises it over his head.

'*No!*'

Hotaka scrambles to his feet. The ache in his ribs is excruciating, his head is in a whirl and his vision is blurred, but he sprints as fast as he can towards the dark figure towering above Sakura. The thug will shatter her skull for sure with that rod of his.

'*No!*'

As Hotaka runs, a dreadful feeling takes hold: he's not going to make it. He's not going to reach Sakura before that hard bamboo rod strikes her head. It will be close. But close is not good enough. The rod will get there first, and nothing else will matter.

'*No!*'

He screams as the thug brings down the rod. He screams as he throws himself through the air, hoping to put some part of his body between Sakura and the rod, any part. He screams as he watches the rod fall, knowing he can't beat it.

But then out of the corner of his eye he sees something else. Aunt Azumi on the verandah. Shouting. *How dare you. She's my flower.* And something flying through the air in a bright blue blur with a flash of red. He's seen the thing before. Yes! The kappa, the little lizard-like creature – made of solid cement. It passes Hotaka and hits the guy in the middle of the forehead.

The brute drops like a sack of sago. His rod digs into the soil right next to Sakura's ear, and Hotaka does a perfect faceplant into a bed of trampled plum blossoms.

He lifts his face from the dirt. The big man is lying in a heap, knocked out, blood streaming down his face. The other two thugs are running to his aid, but stop in their tracks when they hear Aunt Azumi.

'The police!' she shouts, pointing to the end of the street. 'They're here at last. We're saved!'

The men spin around, leap the fence and scamper off into the dark.

'What a great end to a great night, eh, guys?' Osamu says.

He is sitting with Hotaka, Sakura and her aunt on the verandah, slurping at Aunt Azumi's hot noodle soup.

'Are you for real?' Sakura says. 'Your face is bruised black and blue, your nose looks like it's broken, Hotaka's ribs are in agony, I nearly had my head smashed to bits, Aunt Azumi has had her flower garden trashed, and we all feel like crap! Where exactly is the *great* in any of that?'

'It's in what we've got.' Osamu holds up his phone. 'Pure treasure! What we need to win this fight.' He salutes Sakura's aunt. 'Top job, Kita-san. You could work as a film-maker any day. Excellent action, graphic violence, plus pure suspense in that last shot – I don't know how you managed to film *and* throw that kappa so accurately. Our fans will love it all.'

'You never stop, do you?' Sakura groans.

'And then we have that gorilla over there.' Osamu points to the thug tied to the gate post, ankles and wrists bound tightly. The big guy moans, not yet fully conscious, and struggles a bit. 'What a catch. When he tells the police who put him up to this, we'll have enough to close down those big-wigs.'

'Which reminds me,' Hotaka cuts in. 'Where are the police?' He looks at Sakura's aunt. 'Nearly ten minutes have passed since you said they were coming.'

'Oh, I just made that up so the other two didn't finish off what their big mate failed to do.'

The teenagers laugh. 'Quick thinking, Aunt Azumi,' Sakura says. 'You're amazing.'

'Well, I had to do something, my dear. Osamu and Hotaka weren't in fighting condition, and although we girls could probably have handled those two creeps between us, I didn't feel like getting my hands dirty.'

'Pity about that,' Osamu says. 'Imagine if we had them as prisoners too?'

'Will you give up?!' Sakura howls. She picks up a bowl to throw at him, but then stops and stares. 'I don't believe it.' A huge grin fills her face. 'Talk about wish come true! We do have them. Look.'

Shuffling down the street are the two thugs, ankles hobbled, hands tied. Prodding them along with their bamboo rods – one in each hand – is Tarou, along with a bunch of his friends.

'These two want to apologise, Kita-san,' Tarou says. He opens the gate. 'They also have some very interesting information for you guys,' he tells Sakura and the others.

Tarou shoves the thugs through the gate. Then he spins the two bamboo rods high into the air. They cross over mid-flight and he catches them with a flourish.

'Anyone for kendo?' he asks, winking at Hotaka.

# Thirty-three

**'Come, ladies. Your seats await you.'**

Two days have passed since the attack in Aunt Azumi's garden, two days in which much has happened. Osamu's nose has started healing; it wasn't broken after all. Hotaka's ribs are fine, though still sore. Uncle Yori has mended his nets and his runabout. Work is well underway on Aunt Azumi's garden, and she loves her new walking stick. But most important of all is the news that has spread across the nation about the little town of Omori-wan.

There is a gathering at Hotaka's house to view a special report prepared by a Tokyo television station. Uncle Yori is there, as well as Sakura with her aunt and uncle. is there, too, along with his car-driving cousin, plus Tarou and his pals who helped capture the thugs.

Those thugs revealed all. In detailed interviews carefully recorded by Osamu, and later with the police, they told how much they'd been paid by the mayor of Omori-wan, and what they were meant to do for their fee: end the anti-seawall protest by any means – scare tactics, violence, whatever. With that in hand, plus the video evidence filmed by Aunt Azumi, Osamu contacted the News Channel in Tokyo. They grabbed the story and whipped up a national news item.

'We're ready to start,' Hotaka calls.

The women appear. 'You are recording this, aren't you, son?' Mrs Yamato asks as they enter.

'Of course, Okāsan.' He presses the pause button while everyone gets ready. 'I bet the whole of Omori-wan is recording this. It's the biggest thing that's happened here since the tsunami.'

'This way, ladies.' Uncle Yori beckons the women to places directly in front of the television, between him and Sakura's uncle.

Uncle Hideo bows to the women as they sit, and then turns to Sakura who is standing further back. 'You too, niece. Come. I've kept this spot for you.'

She shakes her head, but Osamu pushes her forward.

'Do as you're told, Princess Blossom. Your uncle is proud of you, as we all are. He wants to show you off.'

'That's right.' Uncle Hideo beckons to Sakura. 'You've done something very courageous, my dear. I know that your father and your mother – my dear sister – would both be immensely proud of you. Please.'

Sakura accepts, but turns to everyone before sitting.

'You are far too kind, Uncle. If I have been courageous, I am not alone. My friends have also shown courage and given me support. Hotaka, Osamu, Tarou. Uncle Yori. Aunty Azumi. Yamato-san. You all gave me the strength to keep going.'

'Thank heavens you did keep going,' Osamu says. 'It's because of you that Omori-wan can hold its head high – the tiny town that took on the giants! Come on, Hotaka, let's have it.'

Hotaka presses the remote and the screen opens to a slow pan across the bay of Omori-wan, complete with voice-over.

'*Not far from the city of Rikuzentakata, in one of the region's most picturesque areas, lies Omori-wan. A once-prosperous fishing community, the little town was devastated by the 3/11 tsunami, like much of the Tōhoku coast. Since then Omori-wan has been gradually rebuilding itself at the edge of its beautiful bay, with its forested hills reaching down to the water, and a tranquillity all of its own.*

'*That tranquillity was shattered last week in what has become a battle between a young teenage girl and powerful forces organised by the corrupt town mayor and his cronies within both the construction industry and the shady world of the yakuza.*'

The view cuts to a reporter walking along the marina.

'*Miss Tsukino's campaign touched a nerve in the town, with a massive show of support when she spoke two days ago at a spontaneous anti-seawall protest. But the impact of her message has spread much further, due to a well-organised social media campaign that has captured the attention and imagination of people everywhere. As her campaign manager – Osamu Fujita – explained.*'

Osamu appears on the screen.

'*Messages of support and solidarity have been pouring in,*' he explains. '*Not only from up and down the Tōhoku coast, but from all over Japan and internationally. For example: the number of tweets coming in on Hashtag OurCallNoWall has gone from a modest flow to a virtual tsunami. Only a few days ago Mayor Nakano and Engineer Oshita tried to silence Miss Tsukino, first by having her expelled from school, then with threats of legal action, and even workplace harassment of her uncle. But their heavy-handed tactics failed, and these men have been left embarrassingly exposed. The cat, as they say, is out of the bag.'*

'*How true,*' the reporter continues. '*The cat is most certainly out of the bag, for there has been an astonishing development in this saga. The attempted intimidation of the anti-seawall movement escalated into extreme violence. Miss Tsukino and her physically disabled aunt, as well as two friends, were viciously attacked by thugs. We have exclusive footage of the attack, of which for legal reasons we can only show brief extracts. And a warning: some viewers may find these scenes confronting.*'

Hotaka appears on the screen, narrowly escaping a blow from the bamboo rod of the small thug, fending off a second attack with a garden stake, only to be cracked across the ribs by a third blow. His mother shrieks at this.

The next scene shows Sakura being pushed over, knocked to the ground and stamped on by the big thug, who then lifts his bamboo rod above his head. The whole room gasps.

'Pause it there,' Osamu says, and strides out in front of everyone. 'There's something you all should know. This great footage was shot by none other than Sakura's aunt.' He walks over to Aunt Azumi and gets her to stand up.

'Thank you, Kita-san. Thank you from all of us. Thank you from the bottom of our hearts. I mean it, because what you did here made all the difference. It turned the tide our way.'

The room bursts into applause. Aunt Azumi bows, blushing, and sits. Hotaka resumes the news item.

'*The shocking revelation here,*' says the reporter, '*is that both Mayor Nakano and Engineer Oshita are behind this violence. The three gangsters involved confessed last night, and I quote: "We were told to shut her up for good. Whatever it takes to silence her, they said."*'

'*Well, they haven't silenced her at all. In fact they've given Miss Tsukino a louder voice than ever. And in a neat irony, the mayor and the engineer are now the silent ones. Both have gone into hiding. We believe that Mayor Nakano was caught by police near Tokyo this morning, but Engineer Oshita is still at large. The head office for Capitol Constructions in Tokyo has terminated his employment, fiercely denying any involvement in the whole affair. It has also put out a press release stating that the construction of the Omori-wan seawall will be shelved pending a referendum, and pledging that funds from the project will be redirected to a housing program worked out in consultation with local residents.*'

The camera cuts to a shot of Sakura walking along the harbourfront, her voice in the background.

'*This is a victory for the small people, the ordinary folk of Omori-wan. They will not be denied their right to enjoy the beauty of Nature.*'

Sakura stops and stares across the bay, the camera following her view.

*'It is also a victory for common sense. Like it or not, we are part of Nature, and we ignore that fact at our peril.'*

*It's a surprise. I can't tell you any more.*

Hotaka is lying in bed later that night, trying to sleep. He thought he would nod off as soon as his head hit the pillow. But Sakura's words are still with him. He can't stop wondering about what she said.

Everybody clapped and cheered when the news item was over. They replayed it twice, clapping again when Sakura spoke, laughing at Osamu's hugely swollen nose, gasping when Hotaka was attacked, and cheering at the end. There would have been a third replay, but Sakura said she simply couldn't bear to see or hear any more of herself.

After all the excitement and action of the last few days, everyone was tired and agreed it was time to go home. As they walked out to Uncle Yori's minibus, Sakura drew Hotaka aside.

'There's still something we have to do, you know? Some unfinished business.'

'What is it?'

'It won't take long, I promise. But we have to do it. And tomorrow is our best chance.'

'What are you talking about?'

'Just be ready. Midday.'

'Why all the secrecy? I don't understand.'

'You will.' She smiles, gives him a friendly thump and pulls away.

What could she possibly mean? In bed Hotaka trawls his brain. What was it they still needed to do? He rolls over and punches his pillow. Why couldn't she just spell it out?

There's a tap at the door. It opens slightly and his mother pokes her head through.

'What is it?' Hotaka props himself on his elbow.

'I forgot to tell you. Principal Hashimoto telephoned this afternoon when you were out.'

'The principal?' Hotaka sits up. 'What did he want?'

'He wanted to speak to you. Personally. He asked if he could come here tomorrow morning.'

'Did he say anything else?'

'Nothing else, only it sounded important. So I told him it would be fine.'

'Of course, Okāsan.'

Hotaka remains sitting after his mother slides the door closed. It's going to be a long night.

# Thirty-four

'**No wonder you kept it** a secret. This is amazing.'

Hotaka sucks in a breath, trying to stay calm.

'I thought you'd be impressed,' Sakura replies.

'Oh, I'm impressed. Can't say I like the idea, but I'm definitely impressed. It's not at all what I expected.'

'Sure, but it's what you need. It's what you have to do.'

'That's easy for you to say.'

'Hey, I'm doing it too. I told you: we jump together.'

Hotaka stands at the edge of the cliff that he and Takeshi used to come to all those years ago, Sakura beside him. They've already changed into the thick wetsuits they'll need in the sea below. He looks down. It's a beautifully calm day, the sea almost still. A small motorboat bobs about like a toy in the clear blue water.

'You've even got Uncle Yori in on the act.'

'I had to ask him. He's my lifesaver. He'll throw me a buoy once we're in the water.'

'Of course! I forgot. You can't swim. You are nuts!'

'Don't worry, I can dog paddle.'

'I don't believe this. You must be scared.'

'No. I'm terrified.'

'Then why are you doing it?'

'Because I have to.'

'Why would you *have* to?'

'Lots of reasons. I'm not sure which is most important, but I know that when you told me about Takeshi the other day on the beach, I couldn't get him out of my head. Remember how you said it seemed as if he was talking *through* me?'

'Of course I do.'

'Well maybe he *was. Who can say*? But what I do know is that when you told me those things that afternoon, I realised then that you had to do this. You had to jump. You had to get it over with once and for all.'

'Unfinished business, eh?'

'Exactly.'

'Okay, but that still doesn't explain why *you* have to jump.'

'It's my way of thanking you.'

'Thanking me? For what?'

'For being such an amazing friend. You've stood up for me, stood *with* me, by me, given me strength.'

'So has Osamu. How come he's not jumping?'

Sakura laughs. 'Are you serious? He'd talk all the way down. Anyway, this is about us. You don't realise how good you've been for me. Your support has meant more than anything. This is my way of saying thanks – by helping you resolve this Takeshi thing. See, I don't think you'd do this by yourself, but I know you will if we go together.

That's why I have to jump. It's my leap of faith, if you like, in you.'

*Leap of faith.* Takeshi's words again coming from her lips. Hotaka stares into her eyes and wonders if it is only Sakura talking.

'So?' She is close to him now. 'Is it on?'

He nods. 'Yeah, it's on.'

She takes his hand and they step backwards in slow, even paces, counting aloud. At ten, they stop.

'We'll never forget this, you know?' she says. 'Whatever we do in life, wherever we end up, we will always remember this. Even when we're old and wrinkled, we'll remember our—'

'Our leap of faith?'

'Yes,' she replies. 'Ready?'

'No.' Hotaka shakes his head. 'Not yet.'

Sakura frowns. 'What do you mean?'

Hotaka grins. 'I have a surprise for you as well. I received an important visitor this morning, with a very important request.'

'Go on.'

'Principal Hashimoto came to our house. I've never seen him so polite. He came to ask about you.'

'Why didn't he come to me?'

'Who knows? Because of your fiery temperament? Arrogance? Stubbornness? Uncompromising attitude?'

'Ha, ha.'

'He probably thought you'd have slammed the door in his face.'

'Yeah, and I probably would have.'

'Anyway, he asked me if I'd apologise to you on his behalf.'

'Really?'

'He also said he's writing you a formal letter of apology. He insisted he'd been misled by the mayor and others, and that he should have given you a proper hearing. He sincerely hoped that – and I quote – *you would forgive him and consider the whole affair an unfortunate mistake.*'

'Of course I will.' Sakura gasps. 'That must have been so hard for him.'

'It was. I felt embarrassed for him. But that's not all. He said he would be extremely honoured if you would agree to give the closing speech at the Memorial Concert.'

'What! How come?'

'Your speech the other day at the marina blew him away. He said it made him feel very emotional.'

'Old Hashimoto, emotional? Get real.'

'It's true. He called you powerful and inspiring, and begged me to persuade you to agree to give the speech.'

'But what do I speak about? And for how long?'

'You decide. He said you'd know better than anyone. Pretty trusting, eh?'

'But—'

'Enough! You're the one sounding like an old motorboat now. Cut the buts! Isn't that why we're here? Just say yes.'

She gazes at him for a moment, then smiles. 'Yes,' she whispers, stepping closer. 'And you?'

He sighs. 'Oh yes!'

'Let's do it, then.'

They turn together and face the horizon.

They breathe in together, long and deep.

'The Great Ones are calling us,' Hotaka shouts. He reels off a list of sea gods and water spirits: 'Ryo-Wo! Watatsumi! Suijin! Isora! Mizuchi! We come!'

Sakura shouts as well. 'We come!'

And they run.

They run as one, as fast as they can, past the point of no return, inexorably towards the edge of the cliff, where they throw themselves at the sky.

The vast unquestioning silence of the sky.

# Thirty-five

'**Wakaino!**'

Hotaka turns to see the old Shaman Lady shuffling towards him as quickly as her frail legs can go.

'Let me see for myself.' She cackles excitedly. 'I must be sure.'

'What is it, obaba?' Hotaka has a cheeky smile, for he knows exactly why she's after him.

'Hush.' The Shaman Lady grabs his arm with her bony hand. She squints, focusing on his head and shoulders. She wrinkles her brow and steps back, scanning the rest of his body. 'Yes!' she shouts. 'You're free. The Untethered One has gone.' She grins broadly, revealing a row of crooked teeth.

'I know.' Hotaka laughs. 'It's wonderful.'

Wonderful. He's felt this way ever since he leapt from the cliff, two days ago. A huge load has lifted from his shoulders, leaving him as free as the breeze, as light as the air. And even now he doesn't yet feel as though he's landed. He's still floating down.

Hotaka is outside the school hall. The Memorial Concert for the Tōhoku earthquake and tsunami has just finished and people are spilling out into the afternoon sun. There's a lightness in the air that he feels sure has never been there after past memorial ceremonies. People are actually talking to each other, stopping to chat in groups rather than heading straight home with their misery. Quite a few are even smiling. This Memorial Concert has definitely been a success. The show went off like a dream.

His mind drifts back over snippets from the day. The opening speech by Abbot Etsudo, rich in simple wisdom. The kumi-daiko ensemble, drumming up a storm of rage and rhythm. The storytellers with their mix of comic tales and more serious kamishibai. The poems spread through the ceremony, plus the traditional folk songs and dances, performed by students. The old Shaman Lady, disturbing yet cathartic. And the marvellous Puppet People, their show an explosion of pure entertainment.

But of all the performances, the one that most deeply moved Hotaka was that of the elderly geisha, Miss Kosaki. She could have sung any song and made it special. But the one she chose was perfect – a song about memory and reflection.

*My memories always join me when I walk along the*
*    beach.*
*They're in the little waves that shimmy up the shore:*
*They whisper with the breeze. They're in the morning*
*    sun.*

*Thoughts of people I have known, things that I have
    done*

*These memories stay with me when I walk along the
    beach*
*At dusk they warmly glow as the sun sinks out of sight*
*They sparkle in the stars, as night enfolds the day*
*My memories are my friends that never go away.*

Her hauntingly beautiful voice is still echoing in his mind as he stands outside the school hall. It's like the call of the bonsho, the Buddhist bell, never completely fading but staying with him forever. Perhaps it's like jumping off that cliff, too, wondering if he will ever land.

The geisha was the final act in the concert. When the last note left her lips the audience rose as one and showered her in applause. Not loud, but soft as a sign of respect, it reminded Hotaka of gentle rain.

Mr Hashimoto then stepped forward, bowed respectfully to the geisha and escorted her to her seat. On returning to the front of the stage, he peered at the large school clock, and gave the audience a barely perceptible nod. Not even that was needed. The clapping stopped, everyone dropped their arms and stood solemnly. That time had come, the one seared into all their minds – 2:46 p.m. – the time the Tōhoku earthquake struck, triggering the tsunami that had washed their world away and changed their lives forever.

With that time came its own cocoon of silence in the hall – no ordinary silence, but a mingling of many personal silences. The hall was packed – most of the people of Omori-wan had come – so the sum of all those little silences was deafening, brimful of grief demanding to be heard.

The silence of remembering.

Hotaka heard the sorrow in the hall, saw the anguish and felt the pain – as he had on this day every year since 2011. But this year was different; there was something else in the air, something that had never been there before. He sensed it all around but couldn't decide what it was exactly.

Miss Abe knew, though, and when the minute of silence finished she leaned over to him.

'Hope,' she whispered. 'Feel it? That's what our concert has done, Hotaka. It has planted the seeds of hope in these people.'

Perhaps Miss Abe was right, Hotaka decides as he watches the people flowing from the hall. They have the seeds of hope in them. The concert shifted the focus of the memorial day away from mourning the past to a reaching-out for the light ahead.

But if it was the concert that planted those seeds, it was Sakura's closing speech that watered them, nourished them and made them sprout.

She began softly, a slight waver in her voice.

'My parents died about a year ago. I will miss them forever. They have left a hole in my heart that will never heal. They also left a blackness that I thought would never leave me. But it has, thanks to all of you. You see, this little town has shown me something incredibly precious. It has taught me how important we all are to each other, how much we need one another.

'This ceremony is just one example of what I mean,' she continued, her voice strengthening. 'We've been given something very special here today. We have been given the chance to reach beyond our pain. We have cried, of course, as we must and always will on this day. But for the first time we have been allowed to feel more: to laugh, to marvel, to wonder, to think and to ask questions. In short, we have been allowed to feel what it is like to live again as people of the Tōhoku region.

'The tsunami stole that from us; tore it to pieces, buried it in the rubble or swept it out to sea. This Memorial Concert has allowed us to start reclaiming it. No more dwelling in the past where the sun never shines. It's time for us to leap into the future. Tomorrow can be bright, and ours to own, if we do this together. So come.' Sakura held out both hands to the audience. 'Let's do it!'

*Let's do it.* Hotaka can still feel her hand in his as they stood on the cliff.

The applause that followed Sakura's speech was loud and raucous, boosted by yells and whoops and whistles from her classmates, led by Osamu, of course. Hotaka chuckles to himself, remembering it.

'Tell me, wakaino.' The touch of the Shaman Lady shakes him from his thoughts.

'I'm sorry, obaba. What is it you wish to know?'

'The spirit. How did you break free?'

How? At the time Hotaka would have struggled to say exactly *how* it happened, just that it definitely did happen.

That was beyond doubt. The moment he and Sakura leapt into the vast silence of the sky, it happened. The instant his feet left the ground he was a new person, his old self left standing on the cliff top. A split second separated the old and the new – a pinprick of time – and yet a world of difference stretched between them.

The old lady keeps pestering him. 'Well? How?'

Hotaka knows now, though. 'It was easy,' he replies with a smile.

He's looking across at a large crowd of students gathered around Sakura, scrambling for selfies with her, Osamu struggling to establish some sort of order among the rabble. As if she senses him, Sakura glances towards Hotaka. She shrugs and smiles back.

'A leap of faith,' he says. 'That's all.'

# Author's note

Japan has lived with natural disasters forever, but the 2011 earthquake and tsunami was truly horrific – nature delivering death and destruction on a vast scale, along with nightmare images of nuclear disaster. Those images lodged in my head, boiling up a brew of scenarios, characters and story ideas – the stuff of sleepless nights. So when Lyn White asked if I'd like to write for her new Through My Eyes series about natural disasters, I grabbed the opportunity.

Initially I had real difficulty deciding on the *essence* of my story. There were so many issues that could be dealt with. Feeling overwhelmed, I eventually decided that I had to visit 'the scene of the crime', so to speak. I spent a month in the Tōhoku region, seeing and feeling the effects of the disaster, talking to people who had lived through the horror, hearing stories of fear, terror, pain, grief, courage, determination and the power of togetherness. My visit to Shizugawa High School in Minamisanriku and my conversations with the teachers and students gave me a much deeper grasp of the personal and social impacts of the disaster, and eventually revealed the basic hooks for *Hotaka*.

Travelling hundreds of kilometres through the disaster zone, I soon realised that the region was one vast construction site – endless infrastructure being built, machines growling day and night. In this frantic drive to rebuild the physical world, people were being forgotten. More than three years after the tsunami whole communities were still in basic temporary accommodation while the construction Godzilla surged onwards.

It was as if Tōhoku humans were irrelevant to the forces of government and big business behind the reconstruction drive. And because the Japanese have such respect for authority, plus a strong reluctance to protest politically, that Godzilla was becoming unstoppable. As a result, an underclass of forgotten people was growing in the Tōhoku region, creating a man-made socio-economic crisis that threatened to dwarf the original *natural* disaster.

But that was only half the story, the negative side. I also realised that there was a powerful *positive* force to counter this negative story. The Japanese have an age-old tradition of combating the havoc from natural disasters through local festivals. These festivals are believed to bring communities together in such troubled times by replacing the chaos and damage with peace and tranquility. They are bright, happy events that fill people with hope and the strength to move forward. I attended the Minamisanriku Memorial Ceremony on 11 March 2015, and was deeply moved.

Immediately I knew that my story had to involve the interplay between these forces of dark and light. It would be about identity, friendship, togetherness and community, our need to care for others, as well as our need to live *with* nature and not against it. In essence, *Hotaka* had to be a real *people* story, the kind of story I love to write.

# Timeline

○ **2011 11 March 14:46 JST (Japan Standard Time)**
A magnitude 9.0 earthquake in the north-western
Pacific Ocean strikes the north-eastern coast of
Japan's main island, Honshu. The Great East Japan
Earthquake moves Honshu 2.4 m eastward and
shifts the earth on its axis by between 10 and 25 cm.

The quake's epicentre is 130 km from Sendai in
the Tōhoku region and 373 km north-east of Tokyo.
The Pacific Tsunami Warning Center issues more
than 50 tsunami warnings for the Pacific Ocean
from Japan to the west coast of the US.

○ **15:26 JST (approx.)** A major tsunami hits the
Pacific coastline of Japan's northern islands,
inundating approximately 561 square km in
42 municipalities across four prefectures. Waves
up to 10 m high sped out from the epicentre at
about 700 kph, travelling up to 10 km inland in
the Sendai area. About 90 per cent of the coastal
seawalls are destroyed.

An estimated 18 000 Honshu residents are swept
away and thousands of people are later recorded
missing in the Tōhoku region. Tsunami waves
eventually reach Alaska, Hawaii, Chile, Norway
and Antarctica. About five million tons of debris
is swept offshore.

**20:15 JST** The Japanese government declares a nuclear emergency at the nuclear power plants in the Tōhoku region. More than 60 000 Sendai residents evacuate to shelters.

**12 March** Aftershocks continue. Three reactors at the Fukushima Daiichi nuclear power plant experience complete meltdowns and four reactors suffer hydrogen explosions.

**13 March** Residents within 10 km of the Fukushima Daini and 20 km of the Fukushima Daiichi nuclear power plants are evacuated. Total evacuation reaches about 185 000 as fears of radioactive leakage mount.

Prime Minister Naoto Kan sets up an emergency command centre in Tokyo. The Defense Ministry announces the deployment of 50 000 Japan Self-Defense Forces personnel, 190 aircraft and 25 ships to assist the rescue effort.

**14–15 March** Almost 10 000 of Minamisanriku's population of 17 000 are missing or presumed dead. The death toll in Miyagi Prefecture is expected to exceed 10 000.

Tsunami waves destroy back-up systems at the Fukushima Daiichi and Daini nuclear power plants. Three of the 10 reactors at Fukushima experience partial meltdowns and four suffer hydrogen explosions.

The Japanese government receives offers of assistance from more than 90 countries. Australia, New Zealand, South Korea and the US are major contributors to the rescue effort.

**22 March** The official death toll exceeds 10 000. About 250 000 people remain in emergency shelters in the Tōhoku region. The twin disasters create an estimated 24 025 million tons of rubble and debris.

**April** A magnitude 7.1 earthquake occurs off the coast of Miyagi Prefecture and a magnitude 6.3 earthquake is recorded in Fukushima Prefecture.

The severity level of the nuclear emergency at the Fukushima Daiichi facility is elevated to 7 – the highest level on the International Nuclear Event Scale. About 45 700 buildings have been destroyed and 144 300 are damaged by the disasters.

The estimated cost of the earthquake and tsunami is between $122 billion and $305 billion. Japan's National Police Agency records 15 560 deaths with 5 689 injured and 5 329 people still missing.

**2012** More than 5 000 aftershocks have now been recorded in Japan. Death toll reaches more than 15 850 people with 3 287 people listed as missing.

**2013** More than 300 000 displaced residents remain in prefabricated temporary housing units in Sendai and other tsunami-damaged locations.

**2014** An estimated 100 metric tons of radioactive water leaks from a holding tank at the Fukushima Daiichi nuclear power plant. Reconstruction continues along the Tōhoku coast.

**2015** Over 340 000 people remain displaced. Most of the disaster debris has been removed. The Japanese government approves plans to build about 440 super seawalls up to 17 m in height along the north-east coastline in Fukushima, Miyagi and Iwate prefectures at a cost of over $10 billion. The government's goal is to fortify 14 000 km of Japan's 35 000 km coastline. Nationwide concern grows over the environmental and economic impact of seawall construction and the false sense of security it creates in residents.

**2016** Japan's Fire and Disaster Management Agency confirms an earthquake and tsunami death and missing toll of 22 000, with 2 000 deaths from post-disaster health conditions. An estimated 50 000 people remain in temporary accommodation with a relatively small percentage of town reconstruction completed in affected areas. 160 000 people fled radiation in Fukushima and almost 100 000 are yet to return to their homes.

Nationwide controversy continues around the construction of seawalls as national memorial ceremonies mark the fifth anniversary of the Great East Japan Earthquake and tsunami.

# Glossary

**arigatō gozaimasu**  thank you very much

**bonsho**  bronze bell

**bunraku**  traditional puppet theatre

**butsudan**  household shrine

**chashitsu**  tea room

**furu**  metal brazier

**fusuma**  sliding wood panels that can act as doors

**geisha**  Japanese female entertainers practised in the
   traditional performing arts

**gomen nasai**  I am truly sorry; my deepest apologies

**han**  lunch-serving group

**hitodama**  balls of fire that float, thought to be souls of
   the dead in Japanese folklore

**ihai**  ancestral spirit tablets

**ikebana**  art of Japanese flower arrangement

**jīchan**  grandfather

**jigoku**  hell

**ji shin**  earthquake

**jūshoku**  chief of Buddhist temple

**kamishibai**  form of theatre and storytelling

**kanetsukidō**  bell house

**kappa**  mythical creature said to be responsible for
   luring children into water

**Kashima**  god who tries to restrain Namazu in Japanese
   mythology

**kendōka** one who practises the Japanese martial art kendo

**kiai** battle cry

**kimono** wide-sleeved, full-length robe; traditional Japanese garment

**kitsune** fox

**konnichiwa** good day; a standard greeting

**kotatsu** low table that is heated from underneath; a blanket is placed under the table top

**kote** long padded gloves

**kumi-daiko** ensemble taiko drumming

**kuso** damn

**miso** soybean paste

**Namazu** giant catfish who causes earthquakes in Japanese mythology

**nante kotta** what the hell

**natto** fermented soybeans

**nigete** run, get away

**nori** sheets of dried edible seaweed

**obaba** wise old woman

**ohayō gozaimasu** good morning

**ojīsan** honourable grandfather

**okāsan** mother

**onegai shimasu** a request, used when someone is doing something for you or you are asking them to do something

**Oniwaka** warrior who kills demons

**owashi** great or large eagle

**rōka** narrow hallway around the outside of a house

**sabani** fishing or sailing boat

**samurai** warriors in feudal Japan

**san** honorific used after a person's name

**sensei** teacher

**shinai** bamboo sword

**shu-moku** log, used to strike a bell

**tasukete** help me

**tatami** straw matting used for flooring in traditional Japanese-style rooms

**torī** huge gate into a sacred area

**uguisu** bush warbler

**wagashi** traditional Japanese sweet

**wakaino** young man

**yakuza** Japanese criminal organisation; a member of this organisation

**yokai** monster, demon or spirit in Japanese folklore

**yukata** summerweight garment similar to a kimono

**zabuton** floor cushion

# Find out more about...

### The Great East Japan Earthquake and tsunami

Tarshis, Lauren. *I Survived the Japanese Tsunami 2011*, Scholastic Press, New York, 2013

https://www.britannica.com
Search for 'Japan Earthquake and Tsunami of 2011'

http://video.nationalgeographic.com
Search videos for 'Rare Video: Japanese Tsunami'

http://www.theatlantic.com
Search for 'Japan Earthquake: One Year Later'

### Fukushima Daiichi nuclear disaster

https://www.youtube.com/
Search for 'Understanding the accident of Fukushima Daiichi NPS'

http://fukushimaontheglobe.com

### Seawall construction in post-tsunami Japan

http://www.news.com.au/world
Search for 'Japan's giant sea wall to fend off tsunamis'

https://www.rt.com/news/
Search for 'Japan anti-tsunami barrier'

# Acknowledgements

I wish to thank several people in Japan who helped with this book. In particular I want to express my indebtedness to Mr Yoh Naramatsu for his generosity in time and effort. Yoh-san always replied in detail to my many emails during the planning, research, writing and editing of the book. He organised much of my time in the Tōhoku area, acting as interpreter and facilitator in school contacts, travelling to the region himself to help in meetings with young people. He also secured seats at the special Minamisanriku Memorial Ceremony on 11 March 2015, an extremely moving event. In many ways the essence of this book was affected by Yoh-san, for he helped me glimpse a Japan I don't think my Western eyes would ever have recognised.

I would also like to thank Mr Sato, President of Shizugawa High School, for allowing me to visit his school and talk with teachers and students. Three students in particular have my gratitude for their detailed written responses to my many questions: Mr Ryohei Osaka (17); Miss Misato Abe (16); and Miss Minami Sato (16). And I'd like to thank those students who came to visit and talk after school at Minshuku Yasuragi in Minamisanriku where my wife and I stayed.

I must thank Mr Roy Wheatley of Global Consulting & Development for arranging the initial contact with Mr Naramatsu.

I would also like to give special thanks to: Lyn White for her invaluable support at every phase of this book's creation; and Sophie Splatt, at Allen & Unwin, for her remarkable editing work and tireless attention to detail.

Of the various books and articles I read in researching *Hotaka*, I must make special mention of Gretel Ehrlich's deeply moving work, *Facing the Wave: A Journey in the Wake of the Tsunami.* Her account of the 3/11 tsunami's impact on real Tōhoku people was extremely insightful, and I have no doubt as to its considerable impact on my own book. In particular, I must acknowledge that my inspiration for the old geisha in *Hotaka* – Miss Kosaki – came from the true-life then eighty-four-year-old geisha interviewed by Ehrlich, Chikano Fujima, the so-called 'Last Geisha of Kamaishi' (see pages 82–86; 184–187), a truly charismatic little woman.

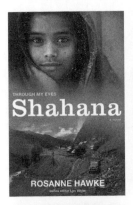
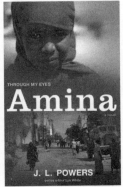
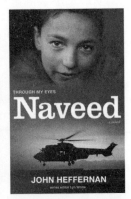
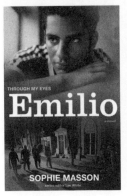
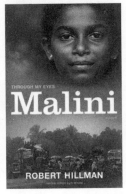

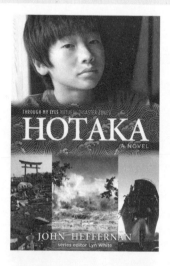

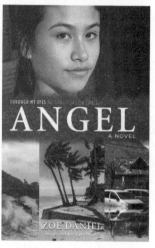